# Day of Fear

A RINEHART SUSPENSE NOVEL

A RINEHART SUSPENSE NOVEL

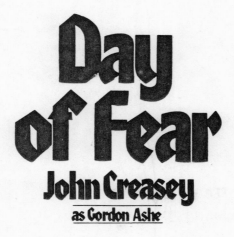

Day
of Fear

John Creasey
as Gordon Ashe

HOLT, RINEHART AND WINSTON

New York

Copyright 1956 by John Creasey

All rights reserved, including the right to
reproduce this book or portions thereof
in any form.

Published simultaneously in Canada by
Holt, Rinehart and Winston of Canada, Limited.

Library of Congress Catalog Card Number: 77-73867
ISBN: 0-03-022396-2

First published in the United States in 1978.

Printed in the United States of America

10  9  8  7  6  5  4  3  2  1

# CONTENTS

## CHAPTER I

## THE YOUTH

FELICITY DAWLISH saw him when he was about half a mile from the house. She didn't give him much thought—no more than she did to the shiny new car which started up somewhere about the same spot, then raced along the road. It went past the end of the drive of this house, and turned towards the village at the nearby crossroads.

The man had just come through the hedge from a road which led over the hills towards Haslemere, which was five miles away. In the valley, out of sight, was the village of Alum. This man whom she had seen in the distance—she thought of him as a man at first—would bypass Alum and, unless he changed direction, would also pass a hundred yards or so away from this house, Four Ways.

The car had vanished now, and all sound of it had gone.

It was morning, and bright and sunny—almost too bright, with a hint of rain to come.

Felicity's mood was quiet. There was an atmosphere about being alone in the house which she rather enjoyed. One could have too much of it, but this morning—well, she could do what she liked, get at the corners which Maude missed, do the little odds and ends of housework which were the regular jobs of Maude and the daily help, but somehow were never quite properly done.

Not that she could grumble about either woman; it was just pleasant to be on her own.

So she thought then.

She was in the bedroom. No shadow of cloud crossed the sun; no shadow darkened her own mood. Downstairs, the radio was on, light orchestral music making a pleasant, distant background. She wore an old, dark-green housecoat, high at the neck, with long sleeves tight at the wrists. Instead of a dustcap, she had on a pink plastic shower-cap, with her hair

tucked neatly out of the way. She had powdered, but not put
on rouge or lipstick; that was another advantage of her
unusual loneliness; there was no need at all to keep up appear-
ances, for she expected no one.

She glanced out of the window again.

The man, still too far away for her to judge his real age, had
changed direction. He seemed to be coming towards the side
of Four Ways. He walked rather strangely, taking a few quick
steps, then pausing, next walking slowly, then hurrying
again. She wondered if that was due to the ground. That
meadow, she knew, was soggy in parts, and the grass was
bumpy. There had been a lot of rain during the past few weeks,
and this was the first really bright morning for a long time;
perhaps that was why she was suspicious of its brightness.
Rain always made that particular field very bad; Mr. Marsh
of Alum Farm, her nearest neighbour—two miles away and
out of sight to the north of here—did not even put his cattle
there after heavy rainy spells.

Felicity turned away from the window, telling herself that
she had too much to do to stand gaping at a stranger. If he
was coming here she would soon know why; and if he was
heading for the village and was coming to find the way, then
there was a good if narrow road from here, and he wasn't far
off his course. There were trees along the drive of this house,
and bordering the road and clustering at the crossroads half a
mile away. Those crossroads gave Four Ways its name.

The telephone-bell rang.

Felicity sprang round. "That'll be Pat!" she said aloud,
and her eagerness was the eagerness of a young wife, although
she was in the late thirties and had been married for fourteen
years. There was an extension telephone by the side of the
bed, and she picked it up and dropped on to the bed, which
wasn't yet made.

"Hallo?"

"There's a call from London for you," a girl operator
said. "Will you hold on?"

"Yes, of course," Felicity said, and glanced first at the
mantelpiece clock, which told her that it was five minutes to

eleven; then she glanced at the photograph of her husband on a walnut tallboy. It was of Pat as he had been ten years ago —and he'd hardly changed. Really fair-haired people didn't change so much, and there was youthfulness in him, now as well as then. In spite of all his protests, she had had the photograph tinted, to show his corn-coloured hair, his blue eyes, his tanned skin. In a teasing mood, he would look at it severely, and ask:

"How's Technicolor Tim?"

In fact, the photographer had caught him in exactly the right mood. Eyes crinkled a little at the corners, mouth puckered as if he found life just a little puzzling, but amusing all the same. Full-face, like this, his broken nose didn't show very much. Felicity often wished she could spend five minutes with the young brute who, many years ago, had punched Pat so hard that his nose had been broken.

She wasn't thinking of that now.

There were noises on the wire.

"Hallo, hallo, hallo," came a deep voice, quite suddenly; and Felicity laughed. It was always the same; Pat could manage to make her laugh, to say the thing she hadn't expected. There was something of the clown, more than the average of the eternal boy, in him. Sometimes she wondered if anyone really knew him; even whether she did; certainly there were moods which she would never really comprehend. "And I'll bet you haven't made up," he went on; she could imagine his grin. " 'Morning, darling!"

"Pat, you fool!"

"Well, you knew all about that before you married me," said Patrick Dawlish firmly. "You can't get out of it now— you wouldn't even in Reno, five thousand miles away." He paused, and his tone changed subtly; and as she wanted. "Hallo, my sweet, how are you?"

"Oh, I'm *fine*," Felicity assured him warmly. "I wish you were here, but apart from that——"

She broke off as her husband chuckled.

"At least you've a nice morning for spring-cleaning," he said shrewdly, "or haven't you started yet? If Maude——"

"Maude's not here," announced Felicity.

"Eh?"

"I've promised her a night and day off for weeks, and as you'll be back tonight I let her go this morning. She's probably in London by now," Felicity went on casually. "She's going to her sister's place."

"How these women stick together," said Dawlish. "Well, manage with Popsy——"

"*She's* not here, either," declared Felicity, and enjoyed the exclamation which told her that Pat was startled and not particularly pleased. He still seemed to think that she was made of something fragile. She laughed. "Darling, I'm *quite* all right and perfectly capable of existing on my own for a day. Popsy's got a feverish cold. Her mother telephoned to say she's keeping her in bed all day, and I'd much rather she did that than came spreading germs all over the place."

At this, Dawlish sounded really amused.

"And our Popsy's fifty if she's a day! What a tyrant that old hag of a mother must be! Well, you'd better catch the afternoon train and meet me in Town. We'll have a meal at the Club or Soho, and drive back . . ."

"*I'm* cooking dinner with my own fair hands," declared Felicity, "and you're coming home, don't make any mistake about it."

"Yes, Mrs. Beeton."

"Before dark, too," said Felicity, firmly.

"I'll be back by about five," Dawlish promised. "Once the luncheon's over, there's nothing to keep me. Incidentally, I have finally decided to say 'no' to the job, in spite of all the allure of position and authority."

Felicity didn't answer; hardly knew what to say.

"Sorry?" asked Dawlish.

"I don't really know what I feel," Felicity admitted quietly. "I think in some ways you'd enjoy it, and I know you'd do a wonderful job, but there are a lot of things to be said against it, darling."

"No Four Ways, London life all the time, all the restrictions that officialdom would put on me—I've decided that it would be a strait-jacket for two and we'd both hate it," declared Dawlish. "If I investigate any crime in future it will be on the old basis of eager and enthusiastic amateur, not as Commissioner at Scotland Yard!" The laughter in his voice was contagious. "Come to think, the very idea's crazy—I'm too much the rebel, too much—but I run on. Breathe easy, darling, I'll remain a country cousin, and next year's crop of apples had better be good. How is Percy?"

"Oh, fine," Felicity told him.

Percy was an ailing pig. The odd-job man had been to feed him and the other whites in the sties, and would come again late in the afternoon. Dawlish was seeking full-time help, but had had none for weeks.

Dawlish stopped talking about pigs. . . .

A few minutes later, Felicity rang off. As always, she put the receiver down slowly and reluctantly; she could have gone on talking to her Patrick for a long time. She honestly wasn't sure whether to be pleased or sorry about his decision. She looked hard at the photograph, wondering whether he'd made it for her. The strength of the face was a measure of his strength of character. M.I.5 during the war, a kind of un-official policeman for years after, a curious mixture of private eye and fruit and pig farmer. At times he had become almost a national hero, and he seemed to attract crooks and crime as a candle attracted moths. One of his closest friends, a Super-intendent at New Scotland Yard, had been known to say that Dawlish had been born to be a policeman.

He had many friends in High Places; one of them was the Home Secretary. He had been offered the post of First Police-man in the land, and—he'd turned it down.

Why?

*Was* it for her sake?

Felicity believed, at heart, that it was chiefly that. The position would have altered their way of life too severely, would have compelled changes which she wouldn't have liked at all. She stood up, slowly, and hoped that Pat wouldn't really mind. She wasn't sure what he would have done had he had only himself to consider.

On the other hand, he would really find his hands tied as Commissioner, and wouldn't like it. His restless, independent spirit would probably chafe under control by the Home Office, by rule and regulation. It was probably the wise thing to do; now, if any case came along that won his sympathy he could tackle it freely, whereas if he had been the Commissioner . . .

While pondering over all this, she had moved from the bed towards the window. As she reached it, she saw the 'man' stumble. Somehow, that shocked her, and wrenched her thoughts from Pat, the job, and his motives.

The stranger was much nearer; in fact, he was only fifty yards or so from the brick wall which divided the grounds of Four Ways from the meadow; just there, the garden was at its narrowest. As he stumbled, he opened his mouth, in a funny way. She could see that he was little more than a boy, and could also see the way his mouth worked—as if he was in pain.

She found herself breathing very quickly and agitatedly, in a kind of sympathy.

The youth staggered to his feet; and 'staggered' was the only word that described his movement properly. For a moment, Felicity thought that he would fall again, and she gasped aloud. But he kept his feet, and stood swaying. He had dark hair, very glossy in the sunlight and set in great, sweeping waves. He had a pale face—in fact such pallor that he looked as if he was dying on his feet. The twist of his mouth told her that he was struggling even to breathe.

He wore dark clothes; almost black, and somehow that added to the effect on her.

He kept his left hand pressed tightly against his stomach. Felicity wouldn't have worried about that except for the flash of crimson at his fingers—bright red, lit up by the sun, the colour of blood.

"He's hurt," Felicity exclaimed aloud.

She turned and flew towards the door and across the landing. As she reached the head of the stairs, she snatched the shower-cap off, and tossed it through the open door of the bathroom. Any other time, she would have called out to Maude or the daily woman, but her loneliness gave her sudden, new responsibilities. The youth was obviously badly hurt, and staggering here for help. There was a gate in the wall, and she could probably get to him quicker that way than by going down the drive, or going through the back garden; but the going was easier the longer way round.

Felicity raced down the stairs.

At the foot, she hesitated. She didn't know much about first aid—just enough to know that if a man was as badly hurt as that man seemed to be, he needed a doctor; minutes might make a lot of difference to a badly injured man. There was another telephone in the hall. She went across and picked up the receiver, tapping her foot impatiently when she wasn't answered at once. Then:

"Number, please."

"Haslemere 012," Felicity said, and stared out of the hall window towards the trees, the shrubs, the grass and the brick wall of the drive. She could just see the gate.

There was a buzzing on the line, and then the operator said, "Sorry, the line's engaged."

"Oh, damn!" exclaimed Felicity. "It's so urgent, I——"

The operator was unexpectedly helpful.

"Isn't that Dr. Scott's number?"

"Yes." Felicity, still staring out of the window, thought that she saw the gate opening slightly. She went on very quickly and still agitatedly: "I wonder if you'd be good enough to ask Dr. Scott to come to Four Ways, Alum, just as soon as he can. Or ask his secretary to send someone, *quickly*."

"Oh, I will."

"Thank you very much," said Felicity, and banged down the receiver and raced towards the door. The catch stuck; it had been sticking for weeks, she kept meaning to ask Pat to do something about it.

It opened, abruptly, and banged against her foot.

As she reached the washed gravel of the drive, the gate in the wall opened as suddenly as the door, and the youth pitched forward and collapsed. He lay very still, half in and half out of the garden of Four Ways, and it was obvious that he wouldn't get up of his own accord. Now, Felicity plucked her skirts above her knees and ran as fast as she had for years. There was the youth, the wall, the soggy turf at the side of the drive, the bright sun and the cloudless sky, all making a sharp contrast.

So far, she had no fear.

•  •  •  •  •

Beyond the wall, just entering the field which the youth had crossed, were two men.

They had seen the car when it had stopped, and the youth had fallen out; in fact, been pushed. Friends of theirs had been in the car. They had seen the youth crawl out of the ditch where he had fallen. So, they had hurried after him.

The friends, a girl and a youth, were still in the car, a Vauxhall.

Had she been in the bedroom, Felicity would have seen the two men heading for the fallen youth. From here, there was nothing to indicate that the men were there.

Just inside the field the two men stopped.

Then one moved after the youth, whom he could not see, although he could see the top of the open gate.

The other climbed back through the hedge and hurried along the roadway towards the front gates of Four Ways. He moved very fast. Something heavy kept banging against his side, as he ran. He put a hand to his pocket and took the 'something' out.

It was a gun.

## CHAPTER II

## THE MAN

FELICITY slowed down as she drew nearer the fallen youth. She was wearing old brown house shoes, which were a little loose, and the turf was so soggy that she kept slipping. She could not see any sign of the injury now. The youth lay on his stomach, one hand beneath him, the other arm flung wide. His legs were stretched out straight, as if he had pitched forward, log-like, having lost all control of his muscles.

He didn't move at all.

For the first time, Felicity hesitated and felt much more uneasy than she had. The sense of disquiet which her husband would have felt almost from the beginning, came now. She didn't like this at all. She looked up and down the drive, but saw no one. She looked through the gate, but the man approaching from the road was not in her line of vision. She might have gone further forward, to see if the field was empty, but the youth made a funny little moaning sound.

In a moment, Felicity forgot disquiet.

She was only a few yards away from him now, and the next moment she was on one knee beside him, speaking in a very calm, reassuring voice. No one would have suspected that she was so much on edge.

"It's all right, I will help you," she said. "Don't worry." She knew that she had to be reassuring; and now that she was here, she actually felt more confident of her ability. Perhaps that was because there was no sign of blood; it was almost as if she had imagined that bright crimson.

The youth made no more sounds.

Felicity touched his shoulder.

"*Can* you hear me?"

He didn't move, and didn't seem to be breathing. Fear for him clutched at her again. There was nothing to see while he lay like this, and the wound was in his chest; chest, or possibly high in his stomach, anyhow. Gently, she put one arm beneath him and began to ease him round, and when she could, she used her other hand to support him. She wanted to be very gentle, so as not to hurt him; she wasn't even sure that she should move him, but had to find out how bad the wound was. It might be only a cut, he might be just exhausted.

She tensed her muscles for the final effort.

Soon, the youth was on his side, and Felicity saw the blood on his hand, which had been crushed beneath him; and blood also on his waistcoat and his shirt.

She clenched her teeth, determined not to give way to the feeling of nausea.

Very gently, she eased the youth over on to his back, and made herself study the wound. It was in the middle of his body; too low for the chest, somewhere about the stomach. Blood had spread over the grass like a huge poppy, and smeared his hand; it was everywhere.

There was no movement at all at his lips.

Was he—*dead*?

Felicity moved her right hand and took the youth's wrist; and as she felt for the pulse, she looked into the young face and felt a great compassion for him. It was not only his look, it was hard to say why his face attracted her so much. There was softness in his expression, a kind of goodness. It wasn't until she realized that that Felicity saw that he was remarkably good looking; his was very like the face of a girl. His complexion was dark, he had long, black lashes, a delicate skin; yes, that was the word: delicate.

*Was* he dead?

.        .        .        .        .

As Felicity looked into the pale, handsome face, the man who had followed the youth across the field moved swiftly so that he could approach the gate alongside the wall. The heavy ground deadened the sound of his approach, and even if she looked up, she would not see him.

The other man had reached the drive from the roadway. They began to close in on her.

.        .        .        .        .

Felicity could just feel the movement of the youth's pulse. It was unsteady and faint, but she was quite sure that it was beating. She let his wrist go. She knew that if she moved him, she might do a lot of harm; so she mustn't move him, but had to find a way of stopping the bleeding. That was the chief task. She had to steel herself to look at the wound again.

She opened the waistcoat, and pulled the coat-shirt aside.

She almost fainted, but by gritting her teeth she beat the spasm of weakness off, and made herself study the injury.

She couldn't be sure, but this looked like a bullet wound; it was small, dark at the edges, and blood still oozed from the centre. She prayed that she had done the right thing by turning him on his back, and she tried to think what Pat would do.

He would pad the wound and staunch the bleeding, of course, and there wasn't really a lot of blood. Perhaps it was less serious than she had thought at first. She needed a towel, water, a sponge—and above all, she wanted the doctor. Hal Scott would be here soon, with any luck; she knew of no doctor in Haslemere who would come more quickly in answer to a summons from her or Pat.

She stood up.

She did not see either of the men, but took off her housecoat and spread it over the youth, then turned and hurried towards the house. She shivered, for she had on only a nylon slip and a woollen cardigan, but she didn't give a thought to what she was wearing; only to the youth. From the open doorway she looked back, hoping that Hal Scott would be coming, but there was no sign of him; no sign of anyone on the roads leading to Four Ways.

She hurried up the stairs, to the bathroom. She filled an enamel jug with warm water, added a little *Dettol*, then a sponge. Next she took two white Turkish towels from the airing cupboard, and draped these over her arm. She put the jug down at the head of the stairs. Keep an injured man *warm*, remember—if Maude were here, she would shout for hot-water bottles and blankets. But with everything to do herself, she couldn't be sure what she ought to do first.

There were rugs in the garage.

She changed her mind about rugs, hurried into the spare bedroom, and dragged the blankets off the bed; and then exclaimed, *"Fool!"* and went into her own bedroom, opening the wardrobe door. She put on a heavy coat, of bottle green colour, and then took two big rugs, one of them fur covered. She draped these over the towels, picked up the jug, and started down the stairs again.

At the doorway, she heard a funny sound. It wasn't quite a whistle and it wasn't quite a hiss. It made her look round sharply when she was on the porch, but she saw no one. Had she been a second earlier, she would have seen one man bending over the youth and going through his pockets, and the other man at the corner of the house, keeping a look-out. He had sent the warning, and the man near the youth had backed out of sight.

As far as Felicity could see, there was the sunlit morning, the steep drive, grass, trees, empty flower-beds.

Soon, she was by the youth's side again.

At the first glance she was really startled, and another twinge of disquiet shot through her, for the housecoat had been moved. It was lower than it had been; she remembered tucking it up to the youth's chin.

Yet—no one was in sight.

Was it the wind? It was calm enough now, only a cold breeze.

Had some animal . . . ?

The youth twitched and quivered, and Felicity made herself ignore her fears. His eyes flickered open. She thought that his lips were moving, as if he was trying to speak; then words came, but they were gibberish. His eyes did not open wide, and it was easy to believe that he was delirious.

"It's all *right*," she made herself say, "you needn't worry, we'll look after you."

Words.

Who had moved that housecoat?

She looked up at the open gate, and then went towards it, bracing herself for anything she might see. But all she saw was the empty field. She did not know that the man who had been searching the youth's pocket had climbed the wall a few yards away, and was now actually in the grounds of Four Ways hidden from her by the shrubs.

It must have been the wind; or an animal; or she may

have dragged the coat down as she had moved away, without noticing what she was doing.

The youth had stopped trying to speak; it seemed to her that she was looking down into the face of death. There was no hint of movement at his lips or breast, and he had a kind of unearthly beauty. She went down on her knees, then began to use the sponge, the towel, the sponge again, until she had cleansed the wound. That done, she folded one of the towels and placed it squarely over the wound itself; but she did not think she need worry much about external bleeding; that had almost stopped.

She felt for his pulse; it was beating, after all, if very faintly.

She spread the rugs over him, and then stood up. But she found herself drawn to him, could not look away; and she kept telling herself that he would be lucky if he came through alive. Did he really have a chance? She didn't know. She had never wanted a doctor more desperately—why wouldn't he come? Hurry, Hal, hurry!

She heard a car change gear at the crossroads, and her heart leapt.

Was this Hal Scott?

She turned round and watched the end of the drive hopefully, just as a car passed. She recognized Mr. Marsh's big old Buick—he would be going into Haslemere from his farm. He had passed before she could call out, and in any case she couldn't have made him hear.

What was the best thing to do?

It was sheltered here. The ground was very damp, but the housecoat and the rugs would help to keep the youth warm. She had heard harrowing stories of what happened if a badly injured man was moved, and there was no doubt that this one was badly hurt. Was there? The bullet must be somewhere inside him; she could picture the little dark red hole, the blue ridges round it, and the pale flesh around that.

But his closed eyes, his gentle face, drew her gaze again. He wasn't English, of course.

He . . .

Felicity saw something which she hadn't seen before: a scrap of paper. It must have fallen from his pocket. It had been trodden into the grass, and the footprint was muddy, but that might be her own. *Might* be. She looked round again, nervously, but even the birds were bold again, and a blackbird was perched on the leafless branch of a flowering currant, looking at her with yellow beak shining and little beady eyes glistening.

She picked up the scrap of paper, and read the pencilled words on it—writing which she knew was continental, the characteristics of the lettering made that obvious. It told a long, long story in four short lines, for it read:

> P. Dawlish
> Four Ways
> Haslemere
> England

Felicity exclaimed, with a catch in her breath, "He was coming to see Pat!"

From that moment on, she felt really frightened.

It was not because of anything she saw, for the two men were still out of sight although they had reached the empty house. One was watching her from the bedroom window, the other searching the room with the swift expertness of a man who knew exactly what he was doing. It was the belated correlation of events in Felicity's mind which frightened her so badly. A man coming to see Pat, shot in the stomach, and staggering across the soggy field to Four Ways.

*Where had the shooting taken place?*

She had not heard the crack of a shot nearby, but that gave her no real reassurance. She realized, at last, that he had been hurt before he had climbed the hedge, but—could he have walked far with such a wound?

Was he being followed?

Her heart began to race, and she was sharply and painfully aware of her solitude. She looked about the field again, but it was empty. She looked up and down the drive, scanning bushes which might hide someone. It didn't occur to her that she should look up at the bedroom window—and even if she had, she would not have seen the man, for he kept to one side and was hidden by the curtains.

It wasn't conceivable that the youth had come very far with that ugly wound, so whoever had shot him must still be near.

That was the main reason for her new fears, which were taking complete possession of her now.

Why—*why* had they shot a lad like this? Who could be so heartless?

The answer to 'why' came almost as quickly as the question, he had been shot in order to stop him from getting here. He had been coming to see Pat, doubtless to seek help.

She shivered, in spite of the heavy coat. Now, she felt conscious of watching eyes on her from all directions; the bare trees, the blank wall, the windows of the house, all seemed to be hiding men. She tried to scoff at herself, but could not. She wondered if she dared move the youth, and knew that she must not, but—she was in desperate need of help.

What was the matter with her? Why had she been so long in realizing that? Even when she had seen the youth fall, she should have guessed.

She hadn't seen the wound, of course, hadn't known that it was a bullet wound, hadn't even been sure that it had been serious.

She caught her breath.

*Could the youth have shot himself?*

She didn't know whether he had a gun; if he had, then half of her troubles and her fears would be over. With a quick revulsion of feeling, she was prepared to laugh at them. She went down on one knee and lifted the rugs and the housecoat, then felt in the youth's pockets. As she did so, she realized how very cold he was—and that she had tried to buoy herself up with false hope.

He carried no gun, so he hadn't shot himself.

Then . . .

Where was the man who had shot him?

Felicity turned away from the unconscious youth, with the scrap of paper in her hand. A gust of wind swept up from the drive gates, and she shivered again, only partly from cold. Fear was back, like a heavy blanket. She quickened her pace, not because she could see anyone, but because she had to reach that telephone and send for help. Even if there was no need, no one could blame her wanting help from the police.

She reached the doorway.

As she did so she missed a step. Provided she had help, it didn't matter if the police knew of this or not. Pat had turned his face against being the First Policeman simply so that he could handle a thing like this in any way that he thought best. There was tart bitterness in the irony that an emergency had come so quickly, when she was alone, but—should she tell the police, or first get in touch with Pat?

Thank God she knew he was safe in London.

She heard a car change gear at the bottom of the drive, turned to look, and saw that it was Hal Scott's green Wolseley. He always left it in the road and walked up, but that would only take a minute. Here was the help that she and the youth needed; it was really out of her hands now. She felt a great surge of relief as she waved to Scott, and then moved quickly to the telephone. Bless that operator! She was answered almost at once, asked for Trunks, and was giving the number of Pat's club before the car was half-way up the drive.

"Please hold on . . ."

Felicity put the receiver down for a moment, stepped to the door, and pointed towards the spot where the injured youth lay. She saw Hal coming, and pointed away to his left. She scurried back to the telephone, but no one was on the line yet. She heard Scott's footsteps, didn't actually see but could imagine his square, stocky figure as he carried his square, black case, and walked briskly towards the youth. So he'd realized what she meant. He would wonder what on earth had happened. . . .

"Hallo, Alum . . . Your call to Whitehall 0165."

"Oh, thank you," Felicity said, and was almost breathless. The call couldn't have come more quickly; everything was all right, she could leave a message for Pat and go out to join Hal Scott in a couple of minutes.

Should she arrange for an ambulance first?

She gave a queer little laugh at herself, realized how near panic she had been, and that she was thinking absurdly and illogically. It didn't matter at all. She wasn't alone any longer, and Pat was just at the end of a wire. The club operator soon answered; and the most reliable man to speak to was the Head Porter, Old Sadd. He was on the line at once; it was as if the chapter of exasperating, almost frightening delays had at last come to an end.

"Yes, ma'am," Old Sadd said. "I know the Major's in the club, he's here all right."

"Oh, good, Sadd! Please find him, tell him it's desperately urgent, and will he come home as quickly as he can?"

Once he got the message, Pat would telephone. Of course he would.

Sadd was saying something in his gruff old voice.

"Then hurry, please," said Felicity, when he had finished. "I can't wait to speak to him myself, but make sure he knows it's urgent. Good-bye."

She didn't hear Sadd echo the word.

She put the receiver down, and felt completely free from fear. She almost forgot the plight of the youth outside, but that wasn't for long. Should she send for an ambulance? That would mean calling the police, too. Hal would know what was necessary, and Hal also knew Pat; he would understand why Pat might prefer not to have the police called too soon.

She moved towards the door.

She heard a sound behind her, but it didn't register at first; she didn't even dream that anyone was in the house. Until that moment she had felt completely secure again. But the sound came again; a footfall.

She spun round.

A man stood at the foot of the stairs, and another stood just behind him. The nearer man carried an automatic. He wasn't pointing it at her, was just carrying it loosely.

"Wha . . ." Felicity began, and then gulped. "What——"

"Please keep quiet and make no movement," the man with the gun said, very softly. "I do not wish to hurt you, if you will please co-operate."

He raised the gun and pointed it at her.

CHAPTER III

## DR. HAL SCOTT

FELICITY stood with her back to the open door, her hair stirring in the wind which swept up the drive. If she could turn and run just three short yards, she could slam the door on these men and could warn Hal Scott; but she felt as if she could never persuade her legs to move again, she was so frightened.

The man with the gun was small, thin and almost bald, with a big head and round skull. He wore a belted raincoat, which was much too loose about his waist, although it fitted him well on the shoulders. His face was pasty, but rather dark—olive-coloured. The man who had been behind him but was now approaching Felicity was bigger altogether, with small features in a round, fleshy face, wearing a dark-grey overcoat and a wide-brimmed hat which he wore to one side. He was smoking a cigarette which looked thinner and longer than the average. It had a much more penetrating smell, too.

"Do not move," the man with the gun said, keeping her covered, "and do not call that other man, please." The 'please' sounded absurd. His English was fluent and he spoke it without any apparent difficulty. He seemed very sure of himself, too, as if he was certain that she would do just what he said. "Emil," he went on, "you go and bring the other man here."

So the big man was named Emil.

He looked at Felicity. . . .

Men often looked at Felicity.

She might be beautiful to her husband, but she wasn't truly a beauty, and yet—she caught the eye. Dressed now in that big old coat, not made-up, and with the wind blowing her hair, she still had the quality which had made Dawlish fall in love with her almost at first sight, and which attracted men as beauty alone seldom does. Yet she hadn't even a Beauty Contest figure. Her appeal was just—something. And because men had looked at her so often and with such open admiration, she had a fair idea of how to judge men from their looks. Certainly she knew how to judge this one.

She had been frightened before; she was terrified now.

Yet Emil did not pause as he passed; just gave her a final glance, and went off. She was quite sure that whatever he wanted, he would take.

As he reached the doorway Felicity realized a strange thing: he made hardly a sound. The hall was of parquet blocks spread with four good rugs, and wasn't exactly conducive to silence, yet he moved silently, and that added to his unmistakable menace.

His shadow receded after he went out, and there was absolute stillness as the smaller man looked at Felicity. He didn't have the same frightening effect as the big Emil. There was nothing raw or crude or outwardly evil about him. He had huge eyes, with dark bags underneath them, looked tired and rather sad. His nose was long and thin, with pinched nostrils; the lines from the nostrils to the ends of his lips were almost droll. His voice was almost resigned, perhaps also a little sad. Yet he had given the command.

"What is——" Felicity began.

"Wait, please," said the man with the gun stiffly, and then went on, "Move towards the corner, please—where the monk's seat is."

She glanced towards the corner, but didn't move; she was far too terrified. The little man's sad eyes narrowed, and that brought a vertical groove between his eyes and several deep lines at his forehead.

"Please obey me." He moved the gun sharply.

Felicity moved sideways towards the corner, watching him

all the time. Her knees were trembling, she felt as if she might fall at any moment. She kept telling herself that she was being cowardly, that she was letting Pat down, that there could be no need for such acute fear, and yet—there was the small, grey automatic pistol in this man's hand, and there was the youth's wound, caused by a gun something like this. And there was the face and the expression of the man Emil.

She reached the monk's seat, and collapsed on to it.

The little man glanced at her, and then out of the window; he didn't care whether she stood there or sat down. Her lips were so dry that she had to keep moistening them, although it didn't really help. Suddenly, she turned to look out of a small window, towards the side of the drive and the wall. She could just see the top of Hal Scott's back as he bent over the youth, but she couldn't see Emil.

She glanced back at the small man.

He was watching her now, although the gun was pointing towards the floor, as if he felt quite sure that there was nothing to worry about. Yet, a shout would warn Hal, and might give him a chance to realize that the situation wasn't what it seemed, was ugly and dangerous. Just one shout— and she couldn't sit here and do nothing, couldn't let him be captured without warning.

*One shout.*

The little man was looking out of the window.

Felicity jumped up and cried wildly: *"Hal,* look out, there's a man! Hal!"

She broke off, choking.

Terror rose up in her as the little man raised the gun and pointed it towards her. She saw that it had a little rubber hood fitted over the muzzle—a kind of silencer. She had no idea what was happening outside, could not tell whether Hal Scott had been warned in time or not; and that didn't seem to matter.

"No!" she screamed. "No, please don't——"

The little man fired at her.

.        .        .        .        .

In that awful moment, when she saw what the man meant to do, yet knew that there was no way in which to prevent it, it seemed to Felicity Dawlish that she was looking at death; as if the gun itself meant death. She *saw* the flash. She caught her breath. It was as if paralysis had clutched at her nerves and her muscles. She couldn't scream, couldn't close her mouth.

Death was so near.

The bullet struck her left arm, half-way between the shoulder and the elbow. The force of it was sufficient to turn her round. She felt the sharp, burning pain. Fright nearly choked her now, but she didn't lose consciousness. She dropped on to the monk's seat, and for a few seconds sat there without moving, in a kind of shocked silence. There was a dull pain in her arm after the first few seconds, and then she felt something warm trickling down; it was her own blood.

She was alive. The man had shot to frighten, not to kill her; to show that he was in deadly earnest.

Had it been worth it?

Had she given Hal Scott a chance to go for help? Would he leave his patient, anyhow?

That was all she could think about; but the way she had fallen on to the monk's seat made it impossible to look out of the window without getting up, and she dared not get up. The little man was no longer looking at her, but was waiting as if he knew that Emil would do what he had been sent out to do.

But *would* he?

.    .    .    .    .

Doctor Henry (Hal) Scott had pursed his lips, not liking it, when he had seen the youth on the ground, but he had not been really surprised. One was seldom surprised by anything that happened at Pat Dawlish's home. Scott, who had a Commando training, a physical courage and resistance second to few, acknowledged that Dawlish was one of the most remarkable men he knew. He was remarkable, even to the extent of being in love with and utterly faithful to his wife—

in thought, Scott believed, as well as in deed. That made him quite exceptional.

Felicity Dawlish, whom Scott knew well, had been on the telephone when he had come here. It was easy to believe that she had been talking to Dawlish, she had that kind of smile on her face; lovebirds, after those fourteen years. Good to see, even if one laughed at it gently.

Now, here was a youth who looked as if there was not much between him and death.

Scott didn't waste time.

He went down on one knee, much as Felicity had, and pulled the rugs and housecoat aside, then lifted the towel. He gave a little whistle; that was ugly and in a nasty place, for every two people shot there, one died.

Scott didn't glance round towards the house, but checked his first impression, then felt for the youth's pulse. Hm. Stronger than he'd expected. But he mustn't stay here, this would soon be fatal. If he could be lifted with great care he could be taken into the house for warmth—no, better have the ambulance here right away, that was the sensible thing to do. Odd business—yet at Four Ways, not really surprising, remember.

He started to turn round.

He heard Felicity Dawlish shout, without knowing what it was, but the alarm in her voice was vivid. He sprang round, and a big man, on the fat side, looking huge in a belted overcoat, with a wide-brimmed hat which made his face look like a full moon, was only a few yards away from him. The man had a cigarette jutting out from his lips, and both hands in his pockets. There was one word for his expression: lascivious.

Scott straightened up and asked sharply: "What is the matter in the house? Who are you?"

The big man smiled with one side of his mouth, without disturbing the cigarette. He had an olive skin, rather small dark eyes, and a small nose and a very small mouth. His features looked the smaller because of his big, fat face.

"She did not do what she was told," he said. His voice was high-pitched, without being shrill, and his English was good but not quite free from accent. "She will be punished, of course. Do not make the same mistake, eh?"

Scott was a sharp-tempered man, and just then he did not realize there was deep cause for fear. He hadn't heard a shot. He was worried about the youth and more worried about Felicity Dawlish.

"Who the hell do you think you're talking to?" he demanded. "What do you think——"

"Just examine the man again," ordered Emil, "and say if he will die."

Scott raised a clenched fist. . . .

Emil took his right hand from his pocket and revealed an automatic. Calmly. He had a very large hand, and the gun was dwarfed, but it looked no less lethal for that. He moved it casually, as the other man had, and didn't exactly cover Scott, although he could raise the gun in a split second; and something in his expression suggested that he would have no objection at all to shooting where it would hurt.

"Examine," he said, "and say if he will die."

"Who the hell *are* you?" Scott's voice had lost a little of its edge.

The big man gave a little smile, and this time it was with all of his mouth, so that the cigarette nearly fell out.

"Emil," he announced simply.

"Who . . ." Scott began, but he already knew that he would have to do what he was told; he hadn't a chance against an armed man. If he could gain time—if he could find out, for instance, whether Dawlish was on the way, or whether Felicity was alone in the house or not . . .

Emil snatched his left hand from his pocket.

His movement seemed as swift as light. His arm shot out and he struck Scott with the flat of his hand, a stinging blow which sent the doctor staggering to one side. He didn't strike again, but all hint of a smile had gone, and he looked as if he would gladly strike to kill. There was rawness about him; the quality of the brute.

*"Say if he will die."*

Arguments would just waste time, and perhaps invite

another blow; or else invite a bullet. Scott glanced towards the house, saw no sign of Felicity and then turned slowly towards the unconscious youth. He felt half fearful of another attack, and was ready to flinch; his head was still ringing.

No blow came. He could gain a little time in the examination, but couldn't be sure that time would help.

Scott already knew the answer to one question.

He turned round slowly. Emil hadn't moved, but stood looking on with those brown eyes narrowed and an ugly light in them. The cigarette had gone, was trodden into the ground.

"If we can get him to hospital, we might save him," Scott said flatly.

"That is impossible," Emil answered at once. "He cannot be taken to hospital, he must be treated here. You will carry him."

Scott's temper flashed.

"Don't be a fool! If he's moved without a lot of care, he'll die on our hands."

"So he is as bad as that, is he?" asked Emil, and fell into a kind of reverie. He moved his tongue from one side of his mouth to the other, and looked at Scott, not at the injured youth. There seemed to be doubt in his eyes, and his words confirmed it. "If you are lying, you will regret it."

Scott flared up. "I don't give a tuppenny curse for your gun or your fist, I tell you that unless we lift him properly on to a stretcher, we'll kill him. The bullet's lodged in the stomach, isn't it? Until we have an X-ray I can't be sure exactly where it is. His chances of living are fifty-fifty, *if* the case is handled properly. If it's not, he'll die."

"So," said Emil, and glanced thoughtfully at the youth. He shrugged. "That would be a pity, if it were to happen too soon. How can you and I lift him?"

"We need an ambulance and a stretcher."

"There will be no ambulance," Emil said, "and I do not believe that there is no way to lift him. We can, perhaps, make a stretcher that will serve." He glanced towards the house, then put out his left hand, clutched Scott's, and said, "Come with me."

Scott started to protest.

"That boy——"

"You make me very tired," Emil said sharply. "Just come with me." He had a grip so powerful that it made Scott wince; and he thrust Scott forward in a way which suggested that he had already lost patience, and that if the doctor really wanted trouble, he could have it.

Scott was, consequently, a foot or two ahead of the man. He was fighting against his raging temper, and trying to decide the best thing to do. He knew that he hadn't a chance to get away; no real chance, anyhow. This man would know exactly how to use his gun before he'd run three yards. . . .

Forget it.

There was Felicity Dawlish in the house. Alone?

It didn't matter how Scott tried, he couldn't keep his thoughts straight. The gunman, Felicity's one scream—and then silence. What did it mean? Had Felicity been hurt? How many people were there in Four Ways? What . . .

None of these questions helped.

The simple truth was that the youth who lay unconscious was very close to death. In hospital, his chances were at least reasonable; here, they were negligible. Yet even here, he had a chance. If, under compulsion, Scott had to lift him, he would use some kind of flat board or, as a last resort, blankets stiffened with boards of some kind; a thin mattress, perhaps. The man who had called himself Emil knew that, of course, but couldn't be sure what kind of chance the youth had if he were to be treated in this house.

Scott felt another surge of anger. It was criminal, it was murderous even to think of . . .

Criminal?

Murderous?

They had reached the porch of Four Ways, and the house could not have looked lovelier in the sun. No one was in sight. The polished parquet flooring shone. Some Persian rugs gave quality and colour. The old oak furniture, much of it Jacobean, had the appeal of real antiques. Scott knew the house well, and knew none that he liked better.

The man pushed him inside.

There was the little man, whom Scott had not seen before, looking as if he had been dried up by some scorching heat, so that all the blood had been dried out of him. His forehead was very wrinkled. He held a gun, and lowered it only when he saw Emil.

Then Scott saw Felicity.

She sat on a monk's seat round the corner from the door, and he could see that she was in pain. She had taken off her coat and was clutching her left arm, just above the elbow; and there was blood staining the pink woollen cardigan she wore; there was blood on her fingers.

Scott jumped forward.

"Fel——" he began.

The big Emil simply shot out a foot, and sent Scott sprawling; he fell almost at Felicity's feet. Then, as Felicity cried out and as Scott tried to pick himself up, there came a different sound. It affected Emil and the little man as much as it affected Scott and Felicity.

It was simply the telephone-bell ringing.

CHAPTER IV

URGENT CALL

"PLEASE find him," Felicity Dawlish had said, "and tell him it's desperately urgent, will he come home as quickly as he can."

"I'll find him ma'am," said the venerable porter at the Carilon Club, which is in Pall Mall, and then he went on, "I know he's here, I saw him half an hour ago and I've been in the hall ever since."

"Then hurry, please," Felicity said. "I can't wait to speak to him myself, but make sure he knows it's urgent. Good-bye."

The porter spoke into a telephone that was dead.

"Good-bye, ma'am."

He put the receiver down slowly and thoughtfully, and looked out of the small hatch from which he surveyed the entrance-hall and a section of the passage at the club. Behind him were racks for mail and racks for hats and small parcels, a ticker-tape machine, and a tea-pot and accessories. He did not hurry, for he was one who believed that the more haste, the less speed; and on the slightest provocation he would say so.

He did not know—he could not know—that it was a matter of life and death.

He looked along for a page-boy, and saw none.

He suspected that if he went out of his office he would espy one who was lazing, like most of them these days. But going out meant bestirring his old limbs, and he was comfortable and warm here. A boy would be along in a moment.

One came, dwarfed by the great columns, the vast ceilings, the seraphim and cherubim on the frescoes, all looking mildly indecorous in a club held sacrosanct for men only, if one excepted two of the main rooms. The page was whistling very softly, almost soundlessly, for he had no desire for a taste of the back of Old Sadd's hand or the lash of Old Sadd's tongue. The top of the boy's fair head came up to the knee of a vast statue of one of the Regency bucks who had founded the Carilon.

"Boy!" breathed Old Sadd.

The page heard the whisper, but pretended not to. He continued to stroll. He was smaller than most of them, had a pink-and-white face, the look of an angel and the soul of a small boy.

He had even less reason than Old Sadd to suspect that the summons might concern the dead or the dying.

"*Boy!*" breathed the porter again, in a voice which couldn't fail to carry to the lad, "go and——"

The telephone-bell rang.

Old Sadd broke off, and looked round at it; and almost at the same moment, it rang again. He did not really like the telephone. He disliked sudden noises and anything, human or mechanical, which he could not answer back when he was here, in his own domain. So he glared.

The fair, curly head just rose above the counter of the hatch.

"Calling me, sir?"

*Ring-a-ling, ring-a-ling, ring-a-ling.*

The revolving doors which admitted the favoured few who were members or guests of the Carilon, swung open. They made a curiously insistent noise; like someone drawing a hard broom along a hard floor. *Sssssssss.* Two men came in, one tall, immaculate in dark grey, carrying bowler and umbrella, the other short, immaculate in black, bowler and umbrella. They were hurrying, and the tall one said:

"Sadd!"

*Ring-a-ling, ring-a-ling, ring-a-ling.*

"Nip out and pay off my cabby, Sadd," said the tall man, swinging his umbrella as if he was leading the band of the regiment which he served with considerable distinction. "Don't give the cabby more than a bob."

"No, m'lord."

*Ring-a-ling.*

Sadd snatched three half-crowns out of a tin near him, kept there for just such an emergency as this, and handed them to the boy.

"Go and pay off that cabby, and give him a shilling tip, you understand. Not a penny more."

"Yes, sir," said the page, and grabbed and hurried. Paying off a taxi-driver was a treat; and one could watch the world going by, the slim, sleek-looking men and the slim, *chic*-looking women, the sleek and shiny cars and the ragtag and bobtail of London, for entrance even to Pall Mall was free.

Old Sadd lifted the telephone.

"Oh, Sadd," said the Secretary, a man with a persistently superior voice, "I want you to go along to the main cloak-room and get General Wiglow's brief-case, bowler hat and umbrella, at once, please. Do it yourself and bring them along to my office. Thank you, Sadd."

He rang off.

If there was a man in the Carilon whom Sadd disliked, it

was the Secretary; if there was a member he actively resented, it was General Wiglow. But both men were powers. If he had a favourite member, it was Mr. ex-Major Patrick Dawlish, whose wife had just telephoned that urgent summons, but there was a disadvantage in members being popular with the staff; the staff could rely on being forgiven for any minor dereliction of duty.

Sadd went along to the main cloakroom.

When he came back, ten minutes later, there were three page-boys waiting, like chocolate soldiers with nothing at all to do; even the lad who had been to pay off the cabby was there, with one-and-sixpence change and a snug recollection of a nice little blonde with swaying hips.

"Boy," said Sadd sharply, "go along and find Major Dawlish, and tell him that Mrs. Dawlish wants him to go home; it's very urgent."

Three boys—all of whom liked, in fact almost hero-worshipped, the great Patrick Dawlish—started off together. Zip! They could not have got off to a starter's pistol with greater speed. This was, in fact, a sport. The one who reached the statue of Vice-Admiral Iggleston at the corner, and touched the chip in his right toe, won the job. The others would retire without argument. Any ordinary morning there would have been no difficulty, but this morning they were only halfway towards the corner when the Secretary and General Wiglow came along. The one was, the other pretended to be, scandalized.

Old Sadd was peering out of his hatch.

"*Boys!*" he hissed.

All three of the lads had the sense to realize that unless they really put up a good show now, they would be out on their necks before the week was out, and none of them wanted to leave this job of his own volition. They drew up smartly, stopped grinning, apologized, stood aside for the Secretary and the General to pass, and then went back to Sadd.

It lost only a minute or two, but . . .

Felicity was in terror, a youth lay close to death, Hal Scott knew the look of a killer when he saw one.

.        .        .        .        .

Patrick Dawlish, who did not even know the man who lay in the grounds of the house at Alum, and did not even suspect that there was trouble at his, Dawlish's, house, sat back completely at ease in an easy-chair. He was in that Roman Temple of a chamber, the Smoking Room. Here, amid the hush of brown carpet, hide chairs, huge candelabra, immensely tall windows, a selection of chessmen and even a few draughts, it was permitted to talk.

Or doze.

Or, at a pinch, sleep.

Patrick Dawlish was not really dozing and certainly not sleeping, although anyone seeing him in his current posture would not have believed that. The cynical would have pretended to mistake him for a corpse, prematurely aged and on terms with most of the morning-nap members of the club. The room was vast, the chair was huge, Dawlish lay back in his before one of the great windows and yet he was not dwarfed; he still looked a big man. Even his enemies would have admitted that he did not appear to be putting on weight, for his *embonpoint* was scarcely noticeable even beneath a flower-design waistcoat. He breathed rhythmically, and without any sound. His eyelids kept fluttering. He was several yards away from his nearest fellow member, safe from snoring.

He was thinking.

In fact, he was thinking of his wife.

Among the things he thought about her was that he would have had her different, in this way and that, ten years or so ago; but now, he wouldn't change a hair of her head, be it grey or mousy. She called it mousy. He was also thinking that he would drive home soon after lunch. From here to Alum Village, where he had lived for many years, it was some sixty miles and, London being London, a two hours' drive. By night or at either end of the day, he could do it more quickly, his record standing at an hour and twelve minutes. That had been in the dead of night—and Felicity had been dozing.

Not frightened.

He stirred, to rub the side of his neck.

A page-boy came in, and hesitated. No matter how

irreverent a boy might be outside, no matter what crude
opinions he expressed about the club members in the staff
room, here the atmosphere awed him. For here were ghosts
of past greatness. There, sitting in a corner with a newspaper
over his chin, was a World War I hero whom even these lads
had heard of. There, distressingly old in shaggy tweeds and
frayed cotton and cuffs, was a Flying Ace of World War II.
Here were fighting men of all the services, boyhood heroes;
some of them heroes of their fathers', too. In the corridors,
in the dining-room, and especially out in the streets these
heroes might be figures of fun. But in the great rooms of the
Carilon, somehow they became heroes again.

So this boy moved slowly and breathed softly.

Yet Dawlish heard him, and opened one eye.

The boy noticed this, and grinned. There was the huge
Dawlish, the Secret Service ace, the private eye, the lone
wolf, the man everyone who read newspapers knew about,
the Big Shot—why, sometimes he even snapped his fingers at
Scotland Yard! And this paragon was sitting back, and
opening one eye. Just one. Seeing who was approaching, he
kept that eye open, and in a way which had the page-boy in
tucks of silent laughter, he watched his movements.

Then Dawlish opened the other eye.

"For me?" he asked quietly; for members all obeyed the
rules here.

"Yes, sir."

"What is it?"

"Mr. Sadd says there's a message from Mrs. Dawlish, sir,
and she wants you to go home."

Dawlish stared at him with disbelief at this most un-
suspected of announcements.

"There must be some mistake," he said.

"That's what Mr. Sadd said, sir."

"Stake your life on it?" demanded Dawlish.

"I . . ." The page hesitated, and stopped grinning; he felt
a little sheepish, but made himself go on. "Well, sir, they
may not be his actual words but that's what he *meant*, sir."

"Hm," said Dawlish. "You know who I am, don't you?"

"Oh, yes, sir, Major *Dawlish*!"

"Glimmerings of intelligence, too," said Dawlish, and then startled the wits out of the lad, simply by standing up. He just drew a deep breath and seemed, *hey presto*, to be towering high above the boy. The boy actually flinched. Dawlish rested a hand on his fair head for a moment, and said, "Let's go and find out where the mistake crept in."

"Yes, sir," said the boy.

They went outside. One of the good things about this giant Dawlish was the way he treated you; he didn't walk just in front or just behind, as if he didn't care to breathe the same air, or else wanted to kick you in the pants. He treated even a boy like a real person. From the oldest servants at the club to the youngest, that was the impression of Dawlish which held sway. And although they were going back to challenge Old Sadd, this boy felt tremendously elated; only once before had he ever walked beside the far-famed giant.

Corridors, columns, portraits of dead hero-members, all saw Dawlish, a vast and massive six-feet-three, stalking towards the chief porter's office, with the page-boy taking two steps to Dawlish's one, and the top of his head barely rising above Dawlish's elbow. When the other boys, for there were now four, saw this, they stood up quickly and their envy was a remarkable thing to behold.

Dawlish drew up outside Sadd's cubby-hole.

"Mr. Sadd, sir," piped up the boy.

"Now, what is it, what is it? Have you . . ." Sadd appeared, grey head, grey eyes, grey moustache, pale face with a scrubbed look. "Oh, I'm sorry, sir, I didn't see you were there! Did you get the message all right?"

"Just what did my wife say, Sadd?" asked Dawlish.

"Well, sir, she *said* she wanted you home."

A boy grinned, and Dawlish kept a straight face. At this point he was only puzzled; it did not occur to him that there might be anything seriously wrong. In fact he was inclined to the view that Sadd had got the wrong member's name.

"That shows how lucky I am," said Dawlish, "but did she say why?"

"Well, sir, no," said Sadd. "I can't say she did, she just said she hadn't time to speak to you herself, sir."

In fact, Sadd didn't quite recall what Mrs. Dawlish had said, because of the trouble with Lord Welby's cabby and the Secretary and General Wiglow and impudent boys; but he well remembered the sense of urgency in her voice.

"Sure it was for me, Sadd?"

"Oh, I wouldn't mistake Mrs. Dawlish's voice," said Sadd in a brighter tone. "No doubt it was Mrs. Dawlish, sir, and I've remembered what she said, now." Sadd beamed as if he had the best news in the world. "She said that it was desperately urgent, and would you go home as quickly as you could? They're her very words, I can remember them as clearly as if I'd written them down."

He stopped, and his smile faded.

Dawlish was looking at him very hard while the boys were staring at Dawlish. What they saw startled them; it was even slightly alarming. Something had happened to him; there was a change in his expression, in his manner, in his eyes. They looked cold; like ice beneath a blue sky. He looked bigger, too; huge.

"Quite sure, Sadd?"

"Positive, sir."

"Thanks. Telephone the club exchange, ask them to get Mrs. Dawlish on the line, and put the call through to the box in the corner, please." Dawlish's voice had become sharp and crisp. He turned to the fair-haired page-boy, but spoke again to Sadd. "Can you let Smithy do a job for me?"

"Oh, yes, sir."

"Oo, yes, *please, sir!*"

"Smithy, nip outside and find Fred or anyone of the porters who can drive. Doesn't matter who. My car's parked in Carlton House Terrace—you know the car, don't you?"

"Yes, sir, that flame-red Bristol, know it anywhere," breathed Smithy.

"Have it collected and brought here, and *hurry*," ordered Dawlish.

His manner was like the elastic in a catapult. Smithy

almost went *twang* and quivered as he shot out of the main entrance, with the other boys looking after him enviously. Dawlish meanwhile stepped into Box 3, which held the house telephone and a prepayment call-box as well. He slipped three pennies into the slot, then dialled a Whitehall number; the Home Office. There was a *tick-tick-tick* of delay before the ringing of the number; next came an aloof operator.

"This is the Home Office. Can I help you?"

Dawlish said, "Give me Mr. Parry-Jones, please—not his secretary, but Mr. Parry-Jones in person." He was calling the Home Secretary's Permanent Under-Secretary, whom he might reasonably expect to get in person without too much trouble. "This is Patrick Dawlish."

"Mr. . . . who?"

"Dawlish. Patrick——"

"Oh, Mr. *Dawlish*. One moment, sir."

Well, someone may have heard of him there, too; there was always a hope. Dawlish looked at the other telephone, as if he expected it to ring at any moment. It didn't. The little *tick-tick-tick* started again, and he had an irrational fear that he had been cut off. The club exchange would surely be through to Four Ways by now, anyhow.

"Hallo, Mr. Dawlish." That was a voice with a Welsh lilt, human and friendly, too. "How can I help you?"

"I think I'm going to blot my copybook for ever and for ever," said Dawlish, "but I just can't meet the Waffler for lunch. I mean, Sir——"

"I know who you mean," said Parry-Jones, as if he were trying to smother a grin. "But really, you know——"

"I do know. Heinous and suicidal. The truth is that something's gone wrong at home, and I have to get back just as soon as I can. Tell him that, will you? And—er—tell him that you and I had quite a long chat and you think that I'm going to be the world's biggest idiot, and say 'no'."

"You *are*," cried Parry-Jones, in a tone which suggested that only a madman could even consider such a thing. "Your answer's *no*?"

"Yes. Desperately sorry in a lot of ways. Of course, if

you'd rather I told the great man myself, just leave it for a while, but if he has to appoint someone for the job pretty soon it might be as well if he is told right away. Don't you think——"

The other bell rang sharply.

"Desperately sorry. 'Bye," boomed Dawlish.

• He put down one receiver with a click, and picked the other up; and that was almost with a click, too. He put the second receiver to his ear, and was breathing more harshly than usual, for anything from Felicity saying 'desperately urgent' could only be precisely that. He knew of no cause for urgency or for fear, yet only if she was scared would she have left such a message with Old Sadd. After all, he'd called her only an hour before; what could have happened so suddenly? It was almost like a hoax.

Could Sadd have made a mistake about that voice?

"Dawlish here," he said.

"Oh, your call to Alum, Surrey, 512, Major Dawlish, I'm sorry but there's no reply."

"*What!*" Dawlish asked roughly.

"I assure you there isn't, sir. Trunks have been calling the number for several minutes, there's no reply."

"Ask Trunks to try again, will you?" asked Dawlish with forced calm, and when she had spoken to Trunks so that he could hear, he went on: "You know how things go wrong, don't you? Did you take Mrs. Dawlish's incoming call?"

"Yes, sir."

"She didn't give you a message, did she?"

"No, sir, just asked for Mr. Sadd."

"Hm. Pity. Well, keep——"

"Just a minute, sir!" broke in the operator, and was gone only for a few seconds; her voice was eager as she came on the line again. "It's all right, there is an answer now, just hold on and I'll put you through."

The fear in Dawlish's heart grew less sharp; in fact, in that moment he could almost laugh at himself. Then he waited, trying to imagine what Felicity would be dressed like, whether she'd made-up, where she had been, why she had called up with that drastic message. Only an hour ago she'd seemed as contented as she could be. But here she was, and relief took the urgency away.

There was still a long pause, and the sense of urgency began to creep back. Dawlish remembered that Felicity was alone at the house, and that might explain why she had been so long in answering; but why should she still delay?

He couldn't restrain himself any longer.

"Hallo, there." His voice was sharp.

"I won't keep you a moment, sir," said the club operator. "If we were cut off, we'll soon get a re-connection. I'm sorry you're having all this trouble, sir."

"Can't be helped," said Dawlish, and tried to sound as if he was really patient. "I——"

Then *Felicity* spoke.

He could not remember an occasion when he had been more pleased to hear her voice, for undoubtedly it was hers. He thought she sounded agitated, but that was all; agitated, perhaps rather breathless, as if she had been running.

It did not occur to him that her breathlessness was due only to great fear.


CHAPTER V

SMOOTH WORDS

FELICITY stood by the small table in the hall where the telephone was. The big, raw man was by her side, with an arm round her shoulders, helping to support her. The small man, unexpectedly, moved across the hall, picked up a stool, and brought it towards her. He pushed it beneath her, and the plump man helped her to sit down; but there was no kindliness in his manner.

Hal Scott leaned against the opposite wall, covered by the small man's gun.

Felicity could hardly think.

There had been the ringing, going on and on, until she

had felt as if it would drive her mad. There had been the tension between Emil and the little man, followed by a sharp exchange of questions and answers; and she hadn't the courage to refuse to answer.

Had she telephoned anyone?

Yes.

Who?

The doctor. . . .

*Did she want to get hurt?*

No, she didn't! She had telephoned the doctor, that was why he had come here. Wasn't it obvious?

The big Emil had squeezed her shoulders, and because of the wound in her left arm, that had been very painful. It was meant as a warning, telling her what could happen if she lied to them. She couldn't lie. All she had to do was to utter one sentence to Pat, to warn him, and whatever happened she would do that, but—she couldn't lie.

Who else had she telephoned?

Her husband. Somehow, the truth was wrung out of her.

Where was he?

At his club; he was lunching with a friend; he——

Was he going to ring her back?

She didn't know.

Had she warned him that there were strangers here?

*No!*

The pressure at her shoulders had come again, and Felicity had felt quite sure that it was both a warning and a threat. Hal was helpless, and so was she; and these men seemed to sense a lie, seemed to be able to tell at once whether she was trying to fool them or not.

*Had she warned him?* It was as if they knew that she had lied, and could read her thoughts. Oddly, she was more terrified of the little man. She hated herself for it, but she just had to tell the truth.

"I asked him to come home at once, said . . . said it was desperately urgent, but I didn't tell him why," she had cried.

"You will answer now," said the little man, in his precise, un-English way, "and you will tell your husband, if it is he, that there is no longer anything to worry about. You will say that you had burglars, but they are gone, and he is not to worry because you are going to telephone the police. You understand?"

"She must say that she *has* telephoned the police," Emil put in.

"Yes, that is better. Mrs. Dawlish, do what I tell you, at once, please."

Felicity lifted the receiver.

She did not know just what depended on her answer. There was the injured youth outside; there was Hal and herself. But if she warned Pat, if she gave him any reason to believe that there was danger here, then he would come rushing, and might run into danger himself. She felt on the edge of panic, and she did not really know what to do.

The little man went to Hal Scott's side, and instead of an automatic, there was a knife in his hand. He didn't smile or frown, but simply said in a flat voice:

"Please obey, Mrs. Dawlish, we do not want anyone to get hurt."

"Hallo, Alum 512," the operator was saying. "Are you there? Hallo . . ."

Felicity said: "Hallo? Yes, I—I'm here."

There was sweat on Hal Scott's forehead; she could see it glistening, like dewdrops in an autumn morning's sun. The sun also glistened on the little man's knife. She could feel the steady breathing of the big man on the side of her neck.

"Is that Alum 512?"

"Yes."

"Hold on, please, I've a call for you."

"All—all right."

She held on, and it seemed for a long time. The hall was still and silent, and there was no sound outside but the occasional shrill call of a bird. With the wind, which was stiffening, coldness crept into the hall, but no one moved to shut the door. Felicity felt as if the cold had got right into her, and that she would never be warm again. Everything was dreadfully confused in her mind. The injured youth, Pat, the fat, lascivious Emil, the sad little man with the forehead which wrinkled so easily, Hal Scott. . . .

"Is that Mrs. Dawlish?" a woman asked.

Not Pat? For some reason it was difficult to explain she had taken it for granted that it would be. 'Long distance' had spelt P A T and nothing else. She needed him so desperately, had almost willed him to come on the line.

"Yes," she said, and there was a moment's pause, and then at last, Pat's voice.

"Hallo, darling," he boomed. "What's all this about?"

Felicity was breathing hard, as if she had been running. She felt the tightening of the fingers of the man behind her, and saw the way the little man raised the gun, as if he was telling her that if she alarmed the caller, he would shoot again; and she knew that he had no objection to shooting. Yet if she delayed too long, it would warn Pat and would alarm these men. If she lied it would keep Pat away and keep him out of danger. She had made the danger for him and must make sure he couldn't be hurt.

Nothing seemed so important as that.

She made herself say, "Oh, darling, bless you for ringing!"

"You didn't expect a postcard, did you?" asked Dawlish, with a flippancy which she knew was put on for her benefit. "What's the trouble?"

She caught her breath.

The plump man's fingers were biting hard into her shoulder, and the little man advanced a pace with the gun raised.

"Oh, darling," she made herself say, "it was so silly, I was scared. I—I heard some noises upstairs, and saw a man in the grounds. I was scared stiff, all I could think of was calling the police——"

"Have you?" Dawlish asked sharply.

"Of course, darling—they—they came, and it was a false alarm. A door banged upstairs, and the man in the grounds was a surveyor or something, it's quite all right. My nerves must be in a *terrible* state."

Pat didn't make any comment.

"Pat, are you there?"

"Yes," he said quietly. "I was thinking about your nerves and their terrible state." Another pause. "We'll have to take a long holiday, my sweet, and I'll make time for it just as soon as I can. That's a promise—I'll get off just as soon as I can."

He was really telling her, "I'm coming now," and that worsened her fears. But he was warned, and he was so capable.

The little man's forehead was so wrinkled that it just wasn't true.

"Yes—yes, do that," Felicity said, "it would be lovely. I'm so sorry I worried you, darling. You—you'll be coming home tonight, won't you?"

"I'll get there just as soon as I can," Dawlish promised.

"I know you will. Be careful on the road, darling, won't you? Be *very* careful. I—I must rush now, I'm all behind with the morning's work."

Dawlish said: "Provided you're not behind with dinner when I get there, who cares? 'Bye, my sweet."

"Good-bye, darling."

Felicity rang off, before Dawlish did, and her receiver rattled on the platform. His went down slowly, lingeringly, but Felicity didn't know that.

.    .    .    .

Lingeringly. . . .

Dawlish took his hand off the receiver only for a moment, once it was right down. He lifted it sharply again, and called the operator, who knew him as a most remarkable man.

"Jane," he said.

"Yes, sir."

"You know Mr. Beresford and Mr. Jeremy, of course?"

"Very well, sir, as club members."

"Good. Will you telephone them for me, and keep trying until you get them? Mr. Jeremy first, I think. Tell them that I've had to leave London very quickly, and I would like them to go to The Bull Inn, Alum Village. Got that?"

"Yes, sir," the operator said quickly.

"Good. Thanks. The Bull, at Alum, where I'll leave a message for them. An urgent message."

"I've got all that," said the operator.

"Fine," said Dawlish, and rang off. Then he began to move fast.

. . . . .

As she put the receiver down after talking to Pat, Felicity nearly fainted. The fat man steadied her, and obviously relaxed himself. Felicity put her hand to her forehead, and it came away wet with sweat. The fat man guided her away from the telephone and then to the front room, and a chair. She dropped into it, gasping for breath now; she didn't know how she had managed to keep going, how she had succeeded in putting up such a good front.

*Were* these men convinced?

She thought so.

They didn't know Pat; they didn't know that from the first moment his fears must have been quickened, didn't know that what he had really said was that he was coming to Four Ways just as fast as the four wheels of his car could bring him. It was twelve o'clock, or nearly twelve, and . . .

The old grandfather clock in the hall struck one.

It was half past eleven, that clock was always a little fast. He'd be here by two at the very latest. Oh, please God, she prayed, don't let him get hurt, don't let them hurt him. But she had warned him clearly enough for him to understand; her 'be careful' had sounded natural enough; he wouldn't miss the urgent warning. But if these men were still here, if they were waiting for him when he arrived, then they might kill him.

Felicity sat with her head in her hands; quivering.

There were voices in the hall. The little man's, then Hal Scott's, then the big man's. She heard movements, as they walked about. She felt too weak to get up and go and see what was happening, too weak to take any chance that they had given her of escaping. She was here alone, there was a window, the village was only two miles away. . . .

She bit her lips, and gasped.

The little man spoke from the doorway.

"When they have come in with the young gentleman, the doctor will see if he can help you. Please, how bad is your wound?" He was coming nearer and speaking quite dispassionately, as if he had nothing at all to do with the throbbing wound in her arm.

She made herself look up.

"I—I don't know. It—it's stopped bleeding, I think."

It had.

"You will come upstairs with me," ordered the little man. "We will get things ready for the doctor. You shall tell me where to find everything that he will need." His calmness was infuriating in one sense, reassuring in another; he seemed to have achieved everything he wanted and he had no personal grudge or grievance. "Allow me to help you."

She stood up.

Her head was swimming and she felt sick. She had the sense to know that she was nearly a head taller than this man, who was little more than a schoolboy in stature; but there wasn't a thing she could do about it. She felt as if she were weak from loss of blood but it couldn't be only that. The man's arm was round her waist, and she felt its wiry strength, had an impression of great strength of muscle.

They started up the stairs.

One, two, three . . .

Each step was an ordeal; she had to pause, grit her teeth, make the effort, then rest on the next step. The little man made no attempt to hurry her; his consideration now was astonishing.

Nine, ten, eleven.

There were eighteen in all—twelve below and six above a half-landing. At the landing, she could see out of the window, but Felicity didn't look, although had she done so she would have seen the youth.

She heard footsteps in the hall; Hal and the fat man were there again; obviously they had been into the kitchen quarters to get something. She didn't hear them when she made for the second flight of stairs.

Fifteen, sixteen, seventeen.

She was quite sure that without the little man's help she would have fallen. With the last step she actually swayed forward, and he pulled her back. He made no attempt to hurry her, but as soon as she took a step forward of her own volition, he guided her towards the open bathroom door. Inside the bathroom was a white-painted stool, and he helped her to sit on it.

"Please, where is your first aid?"

"In—in that cupboard under—under the hand-basin."

"Good, thank you." He bent down, opened the door of the small cupboard, and began to draw out various oddments of first aid; only the *Dettol* had been out before, and it was where she had left it. There was a shelf at one end of the bath, where the man stood all of these things. Finished, he asked, "Where is there some clean linen?"

"In—in the other cupboard."

"Thank you." He opened the airing cupboard door, hesitated, and then took out several pillow-cases, towels, even sheets. He laid these in a neat pile, then ran water into the hand-basin, and said: "I will try to help you. Get up, please."

She got up.

A moment later she was sitting close to the hand-basin and he was bathing her wound. She couldn't see it, but she could imagine that it was something like the wound in the youth's stomach.

*What* had this man called him? 'Young gentleman'?

It was an odd, old-fashioned way to talk.

The little man was gentle, and yet he hurt her. Once she made herself twist her neck so that she could see a little; the wound was not bleeding much, and it hadn't the bluish ring that had shown round the boy's.

"It is not serious," the little man assured her. "I did not intend it to be serious. You see, I knew that we should need your help. Now I shall put some of this yellow ointment on it, isn't that right? Acriflavine. So." His fingers were very thin and wrinkled, like his forehead when he frowned, but he did everything easily and nimbly. He squeezed yellow ointment out on to a piece of gauze, placed gauze on to the injury, and wound a bandage firmly but not too tightly.

"Now, some aspirins, and as soon as we can, some tea or coffee," he said, and actually smiled at her. "Then we shall have the new woman of you! You have had nursing experience, yes?"

"No."

"No," he echoed, and his smile faded. "That is a pity. There is a nurse who lives nearby, perhaps, one who could come and help?"

"I—I don't know."

"Perhaps the doctor will tell you what you have to do and you can help," said the little man. "I want you to understand what has happened, Mrs. Dawlish. The young gentleman, who is very important to some people, has been very badly advised. He was coming to request your husband for some help. Ridiculous, perhaps, but . . ." He shrugged. "That is what he was coming for. We did not want him injured, but it was better that he should be hurt, even killed, than that he should escape and the story should get into the newspapers and become known to all, but I do not need to go into details." He held out three aspirins on the palm of his wrinkled hand, and she took them quickly. "You would like some water?"

"P-p-p-please."

"I will get you some." He turned away, picked up a glass, and filled it. The precision of his movements and of his words was uncanny. She wondered why he was talking like this, and made no allowance for the fact that in spite of his outward calmness, his own nerves were on edge; he was almost certainly talking to keep himself busy.

He gave her the water. "Now, he is injured badly, but we must save his life if we can."

She had gulped an aspirin down.

"But—but you *shot* him!"

"He was shot," the little man admitted; "it was a great pity, but perhaps this doctor can save his life. Is he a good doctor?"

"He—yes, I think so, yes."

"A surgeon also, perhaps?"

"I don't think so, I don't know."

"He has a lot of responsibility," said the little man. "Not many people have the chance of saving the life of an important man, Mrs. Dawlish. We must try very hard. And while we are trying, of course, we must stay here. I do not know how long it will be, but first perhaps there must be the operation and then there must be the rest. I understand that immediately after an operation it is essential that a patient should rest. As soon as it is possible we shall obtain an ambulance and take him away, but . . ." He paused, moved so that he could look into her eyes, and seemed to be demanding a truthful answer. "Are you expecting anyone to call, except your husband when he comes home?"

Felicity had taken all three aspirins, and finished the water.

"Not—not today," she said. "The servants——"

"Ah, yes, the servants." His eyes showed a quickening interest, but no alarm.

"One may come in tomorrow afternoon," she said.

"Before that?" he inquired. "No one at all?"

"I can't be sure that no one will come but I'm not expecting anyone," Felicity said, and there was a fierce edge of urgency to her voice. If he thought she was lying, he might do her greater injury. "Few days pass without some callers, but they usually come in the morning. . . ."

Like *these* men, she remembered.

"We do not want anyone else to come," the little man said. "We shall have to find a way of making sure that they do not. Already with you and this doctor and your husband, when he returns, it will be difficult. But it must be done." He shrugged his shoulders slightly. "You are feeling better?"

Felicity said, "Yes, I—I'm all right now."

"It is pleasing to meet a brave woman," said the little man, and smiled. "You understand that you will not get hurt if you do what I tell you, and if you do not make any trouble. To me it is very important that we should save the life of the young gentleman, and also that we should find out who else he has seen in this country. Also, it is important that we have the documents that he gave you, Mrs. Dawlish."

At first, the significance of what he said didn't dawn on Felicity. She caught only the drift of it. That oddly old-fashioned 'young gentleman' nagged at her. The man spoke of him with a kind of respect she couldn't mistake.

Who was the youth?

Felicity became aware of the change in the little man's voice when he spoke again. She saw him move. She saw his right hand clench, as if to strike her.

"Answer me, now. Quickly. The documents you took from the boy. Where are they?"

CHAPTER VI

THREAT

FELICITY stared into the man's round eyes, into the wrinkled face, at the deeply lined forehead. The worst thing about him was that he could frighten her so easily. From the moment she had seen him he had been able to do that, and when he had shot at her and she had smelt the smell of death he had been able to terrify her.

He did now.

His hand was raised and clenched, only a little way from her face.

"Do not waste time. Where are they?"

She was trembling, her lips were quivering, she felt that she wanted to cringe away from him; but she was already close to the wall, and could not.

"I don't know what you mean," she gasped. "I didn't take anything from him, I——"

She broke off.

The little man's face was closer, now, and all the calmness had gone. Rage was alight in his eyes; rage, and a cruelty which she couldn't mistake. Here was a man who knew exactly what he wanted, and would stop at nothing to get it; causing pain was incidental, whether to man or to woman. Here was ruthlessness in the person of a little, insignificant man, who could suddenly loom in front of her like a giant.

"He had those documents in his pocket," he said, very softly, "and no one but you has seen him. He had two packets, one of them a—what word is it for false?" He hesitated, only to go on quickly: "The dummy. That packet was taken from him, the real one he kept. The documents are not in his pockets now. Where have you put it?"

She almost screamed:

*"I haven't seen them, I haven't touched them!"*

She knew that he didn't believe her, and she was terrified, for his fist was so close to her face, and there was that menace in his eyes. She didn't know what she would do unless he believed her, she didn't know how she could convince him; and she was trembling again in the helplessness of her fear.

Then a man called:

"Otto."

The name was clear enough, and the man was calling from the foot of the stairs. This little man backed a pace. He did not look away from Felicity at once, but said very carefully:

"It will not be good for you if you lie to us, make no mistake."

*"But I don't know——"* Felicity began, and then broke off.

Now she was terrified of this man; more even than of Emil. The sad eyes blazed, he looked evil; vicious. He moved swiftly, and she tried to dodge, but he snatched her good arm and twisted, so that she couldn't move.

"Emil!" he called. "Emil."

"No," Felicity gasped, "no, no, I haven't seen the documents." Her tone, her dread, was piteous. "Don't let Emil——"

Emil appeared at the head of the stairs. Both men spoke in the strange, harsh language, while the grip on Felicity was as tight as ever. Then Emil came towards her. She caught her breath.

His hands . . .

Yet there was something impersonal in the way he searched

her, and when he had finished, the smaller man let her go, then made her stand in the bedroom while they searched; finding nothing that they wanted, they searched the spare room; the maid's room; everywhere up there. And when they had finished Emil said in English, "And I can find nothing downstairs." Then they lapsed into their own language before Emil went downstairs again.

Not knowing what they were going to do made the situation worse. Felicity hardly realized that they had actually searched her.

"Otto," Emil called from below.

The little man, Otto, turned away and went into the landing. As he did so, Felicity had a fierce, desperate impulse. She could slam the door on him and lock herself in, and then shout for help. It would be easy, but . . .

No one was likely to hear.

No one driving along the nearest road could hear; only those who walked, and very few walked these days. Hours might pass before anyone came along, driving, riding or walking. These men could smash the door down; or climb in through the window. It was a hopeless thought, the kind of thing that Pat might attempt but impossible for her.

And her arm throbbed.

*What* documents? What was all this? Who were these people? One man named Emil and another named Otto, and that strangely handsome youth with the dreadfully pale face and the curling eyelashes, lying helpless outside. And Pat's name and this address on a scrap of paper. What did it all mean?

'*Pat, why weren't you here?*'

'But when you come, be careful,' Felicity prayed, 'be very careful; they won't hesitate to kill.'

The man below was calling up again, speaking in a language which Felicity didn't understand. Otto was answering in the same language. He was quite calm now, just a little man who, from behind, wasn't big or impressive enough to frighten anybody. But when he turned round, quite casually and without haste, Felicity's heart nearly turned over.

"Is there a room downstairs where the young gentleman can be taken? For the treatment, perhaps the operation. We do not want to carry him upstairs."

"There—there's the morning-room," she stammered.

"Is there? And is there a large table?"

"No, there isn't, but—but we could take a table out of the kitchen, there's a folding leaf table there that would do, I should think." Felicity found herself desperately anxious to placate the man at least for the time being, to make him understand that she was anxious to help and wouldn't lie to him. She thought, 'Documents,' and there was a catch at her heart, but she got up and hurried out of the room. She went too quickly. Her heart began to whirl, her knees seemed weak, and she put out her good arm to the door, to steady herself. She kept the wounded arm bent; it needed a sling.

The man stood and watched.

The man Emil called something in the language Felicity didn't understand. He sounded impatient.

"This morning-room," Otto called back, in English. Then to Felicity: "Where is it? Is there a couch in it?"

"Oh, yes, it—but *Hal* knows. Dr. *Scott* knows. I—I will get the table——"

Otto called to the man downstairs. Emil spoke again, in English, and Hal Scott answered. Otto put out a hand to help Felicity, and all that viciousness was gone; he looked just a tired elderly man with faded eyes. As they started down the stairs, Felicity saw Hal Scott at the front of a strange little procession. There was Hal, walking across the hall from the front door, holding the end of a door. Then came the youth, lying flat on his back and facing her, so that she could see not only his pallor but his strange, compelling handsomeness; from here, he looked like a corpse. Behind him, holding the other end of the door, was Emil.

They went along the passage alongside the stairs, and out of sight.

A *door*.

Of course, the doors in the house were fastened in such a way that they could be lifted off easily. She knew that as well as she knew her way about the house, but hadn't thought about it. So they had their stretcher. Her mind began to work more freely again. They needed a table on which to put the door—but trestles would do just as well, and there were trestles and a trestle table-top in one of the store-rooms where they kept the apples for short-term storing. Felicity felt almost excited as she told Otto that, but realized at once that he didn't really understand. When she had finished, he said with a frown:

"What are *trestles*?"

"Oh, they're stands, legs, they—but I'll show you!" she cried; and again she went too quickly, her head went suddenly dizzy, and her legs crumpled up.

She fell.

She felt foolish, on her knees in the passage, unable to get up, supporting herself with her good hand on the floor. Her head went round in helpless circles, but it was better when she was kneeling than it had been when she was standing.

She allowed Otto to help her. His arm was hard; steel-like. She felt something cold against her lips, and realized that he was giving her a drink.

She sipped.

It was brandy.

She felt a little trickle down her chin, and wiped it with the back of her hand. Standing up and leaning against the wall, she was aware of voices and sounds. After a few seconds, she felt almost steady again, and remembered exactly what she had set out to do: get the trestles for that door, so that they needn't worry about a table.

She passed the open door of the morning-room.

Hal Scott was looking down at the boy. The door had been rested on the small couch, and was tipped slightly to one side because the ends of the couch sloped downwards. Fat Emil stood by the window, watching them both. Then he glanced up and saw Felicity, and *smiled*.

The feeling of dread that she had felt before was back again. She actually winced, and looked away sharply. She didn't see what Otto did, except that he put a hand on her right arm,

above the elbow, and led her forward. She took him into the
store-room, which led off a passage leading from the kitchen,
and when he saw the trestles, he actually broke into a broad
smile.

"Of course, I remember the word now. Very good, thank
you."

*Thank you . . .*

The politeness was hateful, the worst part about it all; not
really insincere, it seemed to sharpen the horror of the situation,
showed how he would behave if there was not this awful crisis.
But before he touched a trestle, Otto saw a towel hanging over
a clothes-horse to dry. He took it off and, to her surprise, said:

"This is for your arm."

She let him make a rough sling, thanked him, then watched
as he picked up two of the folded trestles, hitched them under
his arm, and started back for the morning-room with the
eagerness of a youth.

*Jauntily.*

Felicity started after him, feeling a glow of real relief; she
had pleased him, he wouldn't behave badly again, would he?
He would believe her when she said that she didn't know anything about a document. He must, because she didn't; there
wasn't a thing that she could tell him.

He reached the kitchen.

She stopped, abruptly, and her heart seemed to turn over,
for she saw something which she hadn't before, and came face
to face with a completely new situation.

She could get away from him now.

The morning-room was a long way from here. One had to
go through the kitchen, into a passage, then into another,
then to the morning-room. She could slam the kitchen door on
Otto, and bolt it; there were small bolts on each side. Then she
could run; she could get into her car and drive off, and could
be in Alum in five minutes.

She must go!

Quite suddenly, she felt as if her mind was beginning to
work properly again, and she knew exactly what she must do;
what Pat would expect her to. Slamming and locking the door

wouldn't really give her time enough, Pat would say. The little man was just in front of her, half-way across the kitchen, holding his trestles and as pleased as a dog with two tails.

She must hit him, with . . .

A bread-board stood on the kitchen table, with a corner of a loaf on it. She could raise it high and bring it down on the back of his head; it ought to knock him out. Give her strength! She quickened her pace, snatched the board up, and sent the corner of bread flying. It was that which attracted Otto. He turned his head, sharply, and let the trestles slip.

He was a split second too late.

She saw the alarm in his eyes as he dropped the trestles and thrust his hand upwards, to take the force of the blow, but she got that blow in first. *Crack!* It struck the top of his bald head with the force of a bullet, and jarred her wrist badly. Breadcrumbs flew in all directions, and one got in her eye, but she took no notice. She didn't hit him again; there was no need to, for he was folding up as if he was made of cardboard.

The trestles were clattering.

Felicity turned and flew out of the kitchen, pushed the door to, and shot the bolt. Up to that moment, everything went perfectly. As the bolt clicked home and she moved way, she stumbled again; the resulting dizziness made her sway to and fro. She stretched out her good arm, and rested it against the wall. She was on the point of fainting, but knew that she must go on, daren't allow herself to be caught.

After this, Otto would do *any*thing to her.

She fought desperately against the dizziness, and it eased. She didn't run but walked very quickly towards the side door of the house—the door which opened on to the paved yard in front of the garage. The green garage doors were closed, and she caught her breath; for she knew that they would also be locked and that would take seconds again from the precious store she had. Scott's car was too far away, she had to race away from the house. Walking or running, she would be an easy target.

If she could keep steady she would be all right. Her arm

wasn't giving her much trouble, although she held it close to her side all the time. The sling was a great help.

Was anyone coming yet?

They would come out of the front door and race round the side towards the garage; and probably they hadn't time yet. She reached the garage door. There was a key in a small recess in the guttering, kept there in case either of them went out without a garage key. She stretched up, groped, and couldn't find it.

She began to cry in her desperation.

Suddenly her fingers touched the key; she stopped crying and held her breath.

She glanced round.

No one was coming. She could see one side of the drive, the opposite side to that where the youth had lain, but the picture was almost the same. Leafless trees, two tall firs at the far end, both dark green in spite of the bright sun. But it wasn't quite so bright now; the morning's beauty was being spoilt by big fleecy clouds which seemed to be riding fast beneath a driving wind. Behind them, in the distant sky, were darker clouds; so it had been a false dawn of fair weather, and would soon rain again.

The wind blew, biting at her legs.

Damn wind, damn weather!

She turned the key in the lock and then pushed the double doors of the garage sideways; they slid smoothly on well-oiled runners. Her little Hillman runabout, a Californian with a red roof and cream body, stood smart and alert as if waiting for her. It was just as she had backed it in last night, ready to leave again.

She raced to it.

If the engine was too cold . . .

She got in, pulled the choke, and pressed the self-starter. The engine woke at the first attempt, then died, then roared again. Everything was going right. She put it in gear and took off the brake and started forward.

As she shot out of the garage, the fat Emil appeared at a corner of the house, his gun in his hand.

CHAPTER VII

## ENCOUNTER

FELICITY had almost forgotten her wounded arm, her waves
of dizziness, even her fears. All of these things had been
swallowed up in hope and triumph; it had seemed to her that
when she actually began to move out of the garage, she was
heading towards safety. These men dared not do anything
worse, once they knew she was going for the police; they
would have to get away as soon as they could.

Now, Emil appeared.

The sun was behind him, putting his massive moon-like
face into shadow. She couldn't see his expression. He was
thirty yards away from her at first, but the distance was
lessening rapidly. She saw him raise his gun. She knew what
was coming, it seemed almost as if she could look down into the
barrel of the gun, but she didn't take her foot off the acceler-
ator. If she were caught now, then she knew that there would
be no hope for her, no forgiveness—so she had to get away.
But in the split second while Emil stood taking aim and she
hurtled towards him, she became aware of other things.

What *would* they do if she escaped?

Oh, they would have to flee, but would they really leave the
youth as he was, or would they kill him?

She caught her breath at the thought.

Then Emil fired.

Felicity hadn't the detachment to realize that he had left
it until the last minute, that with the car coming towards him
he gave himself only just time to dodge to one side before he
fired. She saw the flash, just a white streak against the brightness. She ducked, and swung the wheel towards the left. She
felt the car swing out. It scraped against a bush growing at
the corner of the yard, opposite the house itself. The bullet
smashed into the windscreen, cracking it, but she could still
see through. She felt something spray her face, but it didn't

hurt. She didn't see Emil leap backwards out of the way. The car swerved too far, and she jerked the wheel in the other direction, round the carriage-way and towards the drive.

She heard two shots, sharp and clear, and one bullet clanged against the metal, but that didn't matter, nothing mattered, she was free. There were the open drive gates, the road leading to Alum and to Haslemere, to the police and to freedom. Now she could have Pat warned on the road, he needn't drive into trouble, and—surely they daren't *kill* the youth. They would be afraid of being hanged if they were caught. In that moment of exultation, Felicity felt that everything was clear, and she need have no fears, was free even from terror.

She was only ten yards from the iron gates at the foot of the drive. On either side was the steep bank. The smooth, tarred surface of the road beyond looking inviting. She swung her wheel.

As she did so, a twinge of pain shot through her wounded arm, and she cried out with it and snatched her left hand off the wheel. It was fatal. The car swerved to the right, under the sudden pressure, and the front wing crashed into one of the gateposts. Felicity was flung forward, head against the windscreen. The engine stalled. She felt the car stop, heard the rending sound of a crumpled wing, but that was all vague and far away. She lolled over the wheel, in a daze that was almost a swoon, and was too numbed even to be frightened. She didn't hear the man running down the drive, sending loose gravel in all directions.

It was Emil, by himself.

He nearly pitched forward under the volition of his head-long rush, and grabbed a side of the car to save himself. His gun was still in his hand, but when he saw that Felicity was sitting there motionless, he didn't look at her again but thrust the gun into his pocket and then squeezed past the car and the gatepost, and looked along the road.

No one was coming. Hal Scott's car was parked just off the road, twenty yards from the gate.

Emil opened the driver's door, and pushed Felicity over. She was aware of being moved, that was all. He got in beside her and, for a few seconds, fiddled with the controls. The only other sound came from a fierce gust of wind which lifted dead leaves in a little whirlwind against the windscreen. He started the engine and then turned the wheel, easing the car forward. It groaned and scraped, but he got it clear and into the road. Then he reversed, so that he could turn in—and, as he did so, he saw a big old Buick coming along the road from the right; they were face to face. The Buick was several hundred yards away, and had just come off the by-road which led to Alum Farm.

Emil didn't know that it was the farmer.

He pushed the lever into bottom gear and moved forward, then turned into the drive. Just as he passed the gate-posts, he stalled the engine because of the unfamiliar controls. He started it again, and heard the other car quite plainly; as he moved off the car passed the end of the drive.

.          .          .          .          .

In the old Buick, Robert Marsh of Alum Farm did not see Felicity's car very clearly, it was so far off. He saw her turn back, and actually grinned to himself and thought, 'She must have forgotten something and had to turn back.' When he saw Hal Scott's car he was puzzled, but it was none of his business, and he drove on, humming, towards Haslemere.

In Alum, he slowed down to let a baker's van pass, and as he did so, saw the Alum village policeman standing and talking to the owner of The Bull, Alum's only pub. The village scene was as quiet and peaceful, as picturesque and as reassuring, as village scenes always are.

Marsh waved.

The others, including the policeman, waved back cheerfully before Marsh drove on.

.          .          .          .          .

When the Californian was at the side of the house, its crumpled nose and dented wing pointing towards the empty garage, Emil stopped the engine and sat back for a moment, wiping his forehead with the back of his hand. He moistened his lips, too, as a man might who had just had a very narrow escape. Then he took a slim plastic cigarette-case from his pocket, selected a cigarette, and put it to his mouth. He lit it, and blew smoke out slowly, then turned and looked towards Felicity. Oddly, there was no malice in his smile or in his eyes; There was a kind of grin. Had she been fully conscious she would have seen it and hated it, and hated the way he looked her up and down.

He patted her knee, then gripped tightly—and kept his hand there.

"Very brave," he said, half sneering. "We shall see if you can be brave again." He got out of the car as Felicity raised her head for the first time. He rounded the car and opened the other door and, before she realized what was happening, pulled her out and lifted her. He wasn't really rough. He carried her through the side door, through which she had escaped, and when he reached the kitchen door he stood her down but supported her with one arm, moved the bolt back, and then picked her up again.

The kitchen was empty.

Felicity came to herself to see that, and also to realize who was carrying her, and just what had happened. Yet she was still too dazed to realize what cause she had for fear. Her arm hurt and her head ached, but that was the worst, so far. She was carried into the morning-room, and saw the little man standing and staring at the youth, and Hal Scott by the window.

"Fel!" cried Scott, and moved swiftly towards her. "Fel, are you all right? *Are* you?"

Emil grinned.

"You are the doctor," he said, and put Felicity down in an easy chair. "Yes, she is not badly hurt, there was a little accident." He looked at Otto. "No, we were not seen," he said, "not at close quarters, I am sure. It was a lucky thing, though."

"Is Webber there?" Otto asked.

"I did not see him."

"Or Hanna?"

"I tell you I did not see them, and if I had seen one I would have seen the other."

Otto said, "They are a long time."

Hal Scott was bending over Felicity, watching her intently, feeling her pulse. She managed to smile, and he clenched his teeth because of the pathos. Then he turned round sharply. Both men were looking at him expectantly, and the youth still lay unconscious.

He said: "I'm going to give her a sedative. She's had a terrible time, and——"

Emil leaned across to the box-like bag which Scott had brought with him, and put a fat hand on it.

"She will be all right," he said. "You have other work to do. You have to save the prince's life." He didn't look at the youth, but at Scott; and he didn't speak again, but seemed to wait for some sign of defiance, or else for comment from Otto.

Scott just glared back at him, eyes glittering in his broad face.

Otto said: "If he dies, you will die, Doctor. It will be much better if you save his life."

Scott rasped: "I can't guarantee to save him. The best surgeon in the world couldn't promise that."

Otto just stared.

Emil said: "Then you had better pray. Get on with it, now. The woman will not be able to help you, so I will do what I can."

They moved towards the table and the wounded youth. Felicity saw that they had already prepared; there were all the linen things which Otto had taken out of the cupboard, there were bowls of water, an electric kettle was hissing, plugged into a plug in the wainscoting. The fantastic thing, and in some ways the most hideous, was the calm and matter-of-fact way in which they did everything.

Only one thing had really angered Otto: the documents, which he believed Felicity had taken.

She must be able to make him believe that she knew nothing about them.

She could have screamed.

Then she looked at Scott.

He had changed almost out of recognition, and she knew why. She had seen him look like that, once, after a child in the village had been knocked down by a car, and there seemed little chance of saving its life. An operation, then and there, had been the one chance; and Scott, knowing it, had not waited for a surgeon but had worked—and saved. The look on his face was both strong and yet compassionate. She knew that he was now seeing his patient as his first charge, that no threat would have made any difference to his determination to save this life if he could.

Felicity saw him turn to the steaming casserole dish where the steel instruments lay.

.    .    .    .    .

Hal Scott moved away from the youth, his own face almost as pale as that of the injured man. He stood looking down, aware that Emil and Otto were staring at him, as if they were demanding the answer now: had he succeeded or had he failed? They did not know that he had done very little, for the bullet had been easily accessible. Only a surgeon could help, now— but he had not dared to tell them that.

He looked at Otto.

"We ought to get him to hospital," he said flatly. "We ought to have oxygen available, and be able to give him a blood transfusion. If he dies, it will be your fault, not mine."

"You already know what will happen if he should die," said Otto. He didn't smile or threaten, but turned towards the youth, and rested a hand lightly on the smooth forehead; there was an almost affectionate look on his face.

Then he turned to Felicity.

"Now," he said, "I wish to know about those documents, Mrs. Dawlish. I hope that we shall have no more foolish denials." He actually smiled. "We need not stay here." He opened the door for her, waiting for her to get up, and glanced at Emil. "Go and see if the others are coming," he went on, and he couldn't keep the evidence of anxiety out of his voice. "They are very late, it is now nearly one o'clock."

．　　　　．　　　　．　　　　．　　　　．

In fact, it was a little after one.

Patrick Dawlish was then on the Guildford by-pass, driving with a kind of restrained fury which nearly everyone on the road saw, without understanding; most blamed him. He was, in fact, touching eighty. He wasn't sure whether he had been wise to take the by-pass, but at least it made sure that he wasn't blocked in the accursed High Street, with its cobbled hill and its traffic lights and crowds. As he swung into the town at the last turning off the by-pass, he knew that he would have to slacken his speed a little; but if he had luck with the lights it wouldn't take long.

He'd had a fair run out of London, and ought to be able to take the rest of the journey at speed all the way.

He could still hear the echo of Felicity's voice in his ears. Her emphasis on being careful; her vehemence about being home tonight. He didn't know what was wrong, but knew that it had an ugly menace. From the moment he had rung off, he had moved with the speed which had made his name. There had been the messages to Ted Beresford and Tim Jeremy, through the club operator. The girl wouldn't fail him; and he had dared not waste a moment, but . . .

He wished he could be absolutely sure that they had the message. Once they had it, they would move quite as fast as he.

He had timed the moment of leaving the club perfectly, for the car was actually pulling up outside, with Smithy sitting like a young prince next to the driver—in the scarlet Bristol which was just about the fastest thing on English roads. The odd thing was that none of these people even suspected the forces which were driving him. He was the Dawlish they all knew: brisk, firm, emphatic, pleasant—and then, as now, he had been consumed by anxiety and by his own doubts.

He hadn't called the police.

Should he? That question would nag at him all the time, in different forms, mostly.

Was he doing the right thing by handling this himself? There was no way of telling.

He had rejected the glittering prize of First Policeman because it would restrict him; because at every touch and turn, if there were trouble, he would have to call upon the police for help. There were things which could be done better without the police. Every copper in the country could scream denial at that, but it was still true. But now, with no knowledge of what was wrong except that Felicity was frightened, he had made his decision to drive down here alone and not to tell the police. That sprang from years of working on his own; years of experience, in which he had found that in the beginning the police could be more of a liability than an asset. Normally, he would make the decision to start in on his own, and think no more about it. This was different.

If he was wrong, if this was one of the occasions when the police should have been called, then he had taken a desperate risk with his own wife.

He would soon know.

In forty minutes, with luck; forty-five at most.

Once he was through Guildford and on the Horsham road, his foot went down and the Bristol proved that the hundred on the speedometer was not there just for fun.

CHAPTER VIII

TWO ARRIVALS

So OTTO hadn't changed his mind about those documents, and still believed that she had had them, Felicity realized. He had searched the rooms, upstairs and down, *Emil* had searched her, they had found nothing, and yet they still believed she knew where they were.

What would they do in order to make her talk?

She thought of torture.

She moved in a kind of nightmare, going a pace ahead of him, after he had held the door open for her. At the foot of the stairs she stood still, not knowing what he wanted her to do, fearful of doing the wrong thing. Suddenly, she was less frightened than she had been; it was as if something had blunted the edge of her fear. That little courtesy of holding the door open? As if that meant anything.

"We will go into that front room where we can see the drive," Otto said.

She led the way.

What would they do to her?

The drawing-room was a long one, with windows overlooking both the back garden and the front. The carpet was fitted from wall to wall, a plain dark blue colour, with a flowered three-piece Knoll suit set off well against it, a few nice old pieces, mostly Regency in here, some china ornaments which were precious and almost priceless, and the look which Felicity had contrived to give to all the house: the look of being just right, with nothing ostentatious and nothing really out of place. The wide, leaded windows gave a glorious view, and yet it was not so good as it had been, for the blue sky had almost gone, the sun was hidden, dark clouds scudding threatened rain at any moment. Trees bent beneath a strong wind—which hadn't been there an hour ago.

"You may sit down," Otto said.

She sat down on a small fireside chair with an upright back. Just as her fears were slightly dulled, so were her hopes, and she didn't even begin to think with fierce excitement that Pat would be half-way here by now, just sat and waited to hear what this little man had to say. She didn't know that she was suffering severely from shock, and was in desperate need of rest, of relief from tension.

Otto was doing something. . . .

He brought her a drink, in one of her own glasses; more brandy. She took it, as he said:

"There will soon be others who will help us." Almost to

himself, he went on, "Webber will make lunch, it is past time."
He had a worried, preoccupied air, now, then seemed to brace
himself. He stood in front of Felicity, and spoke to her with
great clarity, as if anxious to make sure she understood. "It
is known that the young gentleman carried those documents
with him, and they were of great importance. I have told you.
He was going to ask Dawlish, your husband, for help. That is
why he came here. When you went to him, he was awake, and
he gave you those documents, just as he had given my friends
the—the dummies. Now, you are to tell us where they are. I
do not wish to be unpleasant, but"—he spread his hands and
shrugged his shoulders—"if you do not tell me, I shall have to
find out quickly. You will be searched more thoroughly. If
they are not on your person, then—but, please, we do not
*want* to hurt you. Simply, we must have those documents and
we shall get them whatever you say, and whatever we have to
do. Why not make it easy for us, and also easy for yourself?"

Felicity said dully: "I didn't take anything from him, and
he didn't give me anything. I don't know what papers you
mean."

Otto stood looking at her.

She saw his expression changing, slowly, much as it had
done when he had first asked her about this. It was as if his
anger and his passions burnt within him all the time, but that
he could damp them down. Whenever he was defied, they
blazed up. He gave her the impression now that he was trying
to keep himself under control.

"Believe me when I warn you," he said, "lying will not
help you at all."

She nearly closed her eyes.

"But I'm not lying, I just don't know."

As he had once before, he raised his clenched fist, and she
flinched back. Something made her open her eyes wide and
stare at him with a defiance which wasn't exactly courage;
was more a kind of resignation. She couldn't defend herself,
couldn't tell him what he wanted to know, so she had to face
it out. Whatever it was, she made him move back, drop his
hands, and snap his fingers.

"I shall help you recover your memory," he said, "or rather Emil will. He is good at such things. Emil!" He turned on his heel and hurried out of the room, leaving her alone with her terror.

Perhaps he believed that she would not dare to try to escape again. Perhaps he had no experience of holding prisoners, and too easily forgot that they would try to get away. Whatever the cause, he went out and for a moment Felicity felt her fears recede, felt a flash of excitement like the one when she had struck him and run away.

She actually stood up.

Her legs wouldn't carry her, and she realized that she had no longer a chance. Of course, Otto knew that. He had been wrong the first time, but felt quite sure that there was no fear of her trying to escape again.

"Emil!" he called.

Emil would still be in the morning-room, with Hal Scott and the unconscious youth. Emil, with that raking look, that rawness, that . . .

What would happen if the youth *did* die?

Would they kill her?

A new sound cut across her thoughts, and she was startled enough to turn her head and look out of the window. Her heart leapt wildly, and hope rose for the first time since she had been brought back. A car was turning into the drive. She put her hands on the arms of her chair, and stood up. In this new flush of excitement, she was able to stand without faltering. She moved towards the window, staring at the car and trying to recognize it. Who might come? It wasn't Pat, it couldn't be Pat; but perhaps a tradesman, or a friend from Haslemere, or . . .

She caught her breath.

Otto had come back, and stood at one side of the window, looking out although standing in such a position that he could not be seen. And his right hand was out of his pocket, with the silenced automatic pistol showing in it.

Of course it was.

And Emil, also armed, would be waiting and watching

from another window. No one who came here would be safe;
no more than Hal Scott had been. Friends would walk into a
trap without the slightest warning. She had tried to warn Hal
and knew what would happen if she tried to warn anyone else,
but how could she stand here doing nothing? Whatever the
risk she would have to cry out.

She heard Emil.

"It is all right," he called from the hall, "it is Hanna and
Webber."

All Felicity realized was that the new arrivals were friends
of these two men.

·     ·     ·     ·     ·

The car was a green Vauxhall, one of the very shiny new
ones. It came slowly up the drive, as if the driver was being
very cautious, and instead of taking the Englishman's natural
swing to the left, it took the right one round the carriageway
in front of the house. But it drew up squarely outside the open
front door.

Felicity watched.

On this, the passenger's side, the car door opened and a
girl climbed out. She was on the small side, Felicity saw; small
but not tiny. She had a nice figure; when her long, grey
travelling coat opened and showed a two-piece suit, it also
revealed that. Beautiful legs, too. Felicity didn't see her face
at first. She was wearing a tweed hat, rather a shapeless one,
and it was pulled down on one side. As this newcomer turned
from the car it was this side of her face which was turned
towards Felicity, and hid her profile. The girl moved very
smoothly.

A young man joined her from the other side of the car.
He was much taller, dressed in a belted coat like all of these
men, and his hair was almost black, his face very pale. He
wasn't bad-looking, but nothing like the 'young gentleman'.
Four other men were squeezed into the back of the car and
these got out quickly. All were small men, pale like the
wounded youth. They stood waiting, obviously for orders.

Otto gave these, in the language which Felicity did not understand; in fact it was a Slav dialect.

The men moved off to different parts of the grounds, and
it was obvious that they were guards. What *was* all this?
They weren't criminals, not in the ordinary sense; not gang-
sters. One man went to a small summer-house, and took up his
position there, not far from the garage. The others, after talking
among themselves, selected spots which enabled them to
watch all the ways of approach to Four Ways.

Otto, the girl and the tall, thin man with the belted coat,
now ignored these four. The two newcomers went into the
house, and Otto turned to Felicity.

"Come, please," he said with that odd courtesy.

He took her arm.

Emil was greeting the newcomers in the hall, his voice
booming out, his laughter echoing. He looked much more
human. As Felicity entered the hall from the drawing-room, she
saw him patting the youth's shoulder. Then, he placed his
hands on the girl's arms, just above the elbows, and gripped
tightly, as if delighted to see her. He stared into the face which
was still hidden from Felicity, and there was the laughter of
satisfaction in his voice.

"Welcome, Hanna, very welcome. You found them
without difficulty, eh?"

Hanna said, "Oh, yes, they had caught the train and were
waiting."

Her voice was quite clear of accent. It wasn't at all affected,
just that of a girl from a good English school, one who had
probably 'finished' in Paris. It was cool, and suggested poise,
like her manner and her figure. She showed no great enthusi-
asm at Emil's welcome, but turned towards Otto. Her smile as
she saw him seemed genuine and warm. Felicity drew in a
sharp breath. Any man who saw this girl would be both
startled and tremendously impressed. Beautiful? That wasn't
quite the word. She had a quality which one couldn't miss,
a fresh loveliness which was sharply at variance with all that
had happened here. And she was so natural as she came
forward, with her hands outstretched. Her *hands*; that was

the gesture which somehow wasn't quite English; few English-women would hold out both hands.

Otto gripped them.

"Hanna, so good it is to see you."

He spoke, as Emil had, as if he had been afraid that she would not come—and was welcoming her home; Felicity's home! They had taken the house over completely, and did not appear to have the slightest doubt that they would be able to maintain control. Emil and the tall young man with the shimmering black hair were talking briskly, almost excitedly, and the girl Hanna looked at Felicity, without hostility and without any particular friendliness. She glanced at the pink cardigan Felicity wore, with one sleeve hanging loose, because of the bandages at her arm, but she asked no questions.

Otto said: "This is Mrs. Dawlish, Hanna. Mrs. Dawlish, this is—Miss Hanna." He gave the impression that for a moment he had been going to use some other name.

Hanna said, "Dawlish's *wife*?"

"Yes."

Hanna's interest sharpened. She looked Felicity up and down, and seemed now to take on a kind of arrogance. Regal? Felicity inclined her head, somehow rebuffed and put out. Hanna turned back to Otto and drew off her gloves.

The tall young man came over.

"Ah, Webber," said Otto. He did not shake hands, and obviously the newcomer didn't expect him to. "I am glad you arrived without trouble, it is very good. Now, we are all hungry. Mrs. Dawlish will help you in the kitchen, I am sure, and there will be plenty of food. Isn't it so, Mrs. Dawlish?"

There was a long pause; much longer than usual, long enough to make all of them take notice of Felicity's silence. Then, when Otto was about to speak again, Felicity said, very quietly and slowly, "If you want any food, you must go and get it."

Otto spread his hands.

Emil was giving that wolfish grin.

The girl, Hanna, seemed even more aloof and arrogant than when she had first heard who Felicity was.

Otto said sharply and with a clear note of irritation: "Already you have been very difficult; do not make the situation worse. Show Webber what food there is, and help him prepare for lunch."

Felicity moved back towards the stairs.

She didn't know what possessed her, and probably never would. Perhaps it was the calm, arrogant way in which the others had taken possession. Perhaps it was the fear of what would happen to Dawlish, a fear which killed her better judgment and made her take risks, as if she were drawing fire on herself. Perhaps it was that her nerves just couldn't take any more without some kind of outlet. She didn't know She simply felt the words welling up in her mind, and they came so strongly that she couldn't keep them down. And she didn't try to. She didn't raise her voice, but kept it on the same level all the time. She looked at Otto, but was aware of the others looking at her, the tall Webber with surprise, the girl without expression, and Emil with a grin which began to fade. Otto kept quite expressionless.

"No, I will not show Webber or anyone else where the food is, and I will not help him to prepare for lunch. You can say what you like and do what you like, but I won't lift a hand to help you. Whether that boy dies or not, you're all murderers at heart. You drive him to despair, you shoot and nearly kill him, you come to my house and take possession, and behave as if it was your own—as if I was your servant.

"Well, I'm *not*.

"You shoot me, you threaten me and the only man who can really help the boy—you treat Dr. Scott as if he was a slave and as if you were his masters. You—*he*," she amended swiftly, and snatched a glance at Emil and waved a hand contemptuously at him—"tried to shoot and kill me. Perhaps he will again. Perhaps you'll kill anyone who comes unsuspectingly to this house expecting to find me. I can't *stop* you. I would cheerfully watch all of you being hanged, but I can't stop you doing what you will. I've tried and I can't do anything more, but—I won't feed you. I won't lift a hand to help you. If I can find a way, I'll help the police to find you. I'll do anything I can for the boy you shot, but apart from that I won't lift a finger, and nothing you can do can make me. *Nothing.*"

She turned round on that last word.

In full view of all of them, she started up the stairs.

She was glad that she could turn her back on them; for had she still faced them, they would have been bound to see the way she broke down; how her lips twisted and worked as soon as she finished, as soon as the effort was over. She wanted to run, to race to her room, to lock the door and fling herself on the bed. She felt at the absolute depths of despair. But she hated them all. She hated each one of them; this girl Hanna as much as any of the men. More. She wouldn't lift a finger to help them, whatever they did to make her.

She reached the half-landing.

Could she—*could* she hold out, if they really meant to break her spirit?

Where was Pat?

Oh, if only he was here!

Felicity moved up the shorter flight of stairs, her ears strained to catch any sound of pursuit. She heard nothing, until one of the men said something in the language she didn't understand. The girl Hanna answered. A man's footsteps sounded on the stairs—and the girl called out sharply.

Felicity reached the main landing.

There seemed to be some kind of argument going on down there, but somehow it didn't matter. The door of her bedroom was wide open, welcoming her. There was Pat's photograph, as if he himself was standing in the room, looking at her. The argument still went on; and then a voice rose sharply, as if on a note of alarm.

It was Emil's.

He came bounding to the stairs.

"Is that true? Is he coming here *now*?" He leapt the stairs three at a time, and Felicity felt a paralysis gripping her, could not move even to the false security of her room. "Is Dawlish on his way here now?" Emil demanded, and gripped her shoulder and pulled her round. *"Is he?"*

He wasn't grinning now; he looked as if he could kill.

．　　　．　　　．　　　．　　　．

How had they found out?

What would they do to her, if she refused to talk?

What would they do to Pat, when he arrived?

There were the men in the grounds, and she felt sure that they were armed; that their task was to make sure that no one caught the others by surprise.

Would they shoot?

Would they *kill* Pat?

CHAPTER IX

BLIND DAWLISH

DAWLISH swung off the main London-Horsham road, not far from Guildford, for the cross-country road to Alum. It was narrow but fairly straight, and there would be little traffic. There was only one small village on this road between here and Alum, with a one-man garage where he often filled up. He hated the thought of delay, but would have to fill up there now; the gauge was quivering close to empty, and at the speed he had come he had eaten the fuel. He didn't slacken, now. He was driving into a stiff wind, which bowled past the car, and smacked against the windscreen. The hedges on either side seemed to vanish behind him. There were no telegraph poles or wires here; just the countryside, some wooded, some meadowland, little of it tilled, with cattle grazing, and a clamour of rooks flying round and round in their endless circles. The sky was overcast, now; it wasn't actually raining but it wasn't likely to be long before it started.

He was seven miles from Alum.

He need not touch the village or Haslemere, this way, but could drive past the road to Alum Farm. He couldn't make up his mind. Direct or indirect approach—which was the wiser? He had come to one realization which he'd over-ridden at first: danger to Felicity could easily distort his judgment.

What *kind* of danger?

One thing was as clear as the sharp edge of blue sky in the distance. There was something odd at Four Ways. Felicity would not have talked as she had unless that was true. He had taken it for granted that someone had been listening-in on the extension telephone, that was why he had said so little; but lines were there to read between and nothing that had happened had given him the slightest cause for relief.

First—Felicity had been so frightened that she had telephoned that urgent message for him.

Second—when he had telephoned her, she had not dared to tell him the truth. That could only mean that someone was there, threatening; menacing.

He had fought the other battle over and over again; whether to send for the police or whether to manage on his own. Now, as he shot the Bristol towards Alum, which was only five minutes' drive away, he knew that he had been right. The others, his friends, had been warned to go to Alum. He could leave a message at The Bull for them. The thing he mustn't do was to raise any kind of alarm until he knew what was happening at Four Ways. Felicity on her own didn't have a chance; if he were there, he could make some kind of chance, whatever the odds.

First, then, he must go into Alum village, and leave the message at The Bull. Then he must get into Four Ways as fast as man could go.

The frightening possibility was that Felicity might already be hurt.

His foot kept right down.

He would come to fork roads, soon, and if he took the left it would lead to Alum Farm and, a little farther on, to Four Ways. The right road led straight to Alum. Alum, first, remember; and he must think up some kind of message to leave for the others when they reached The Bull. He realized, now, how completely choked he had been with the danger to Felicity, how that had blinded him to everything else.

He had recovered his sight and his wits in time.

At moments, he wondered whether he should have called the police, but it was too late, and he persuaded himself that his way was the best way. But if he were wrong, if he were too late to help Felicity . . .

He did not let himself dwell on that.

He could just see the red roof of the farmhouse, and the trees which hid Four Ways from sight. The temptation to go straight on to Four Ways first was almost overwhelming. He beat it, and took the right fork. Soon, he could see the square tower of Alum church, with its nine-hundred-years-old stone and its four-hundred-years-old church clock; and as he did so, he saw Marsh's Buick come out of the parking-place of The Bull. Marsh had been in for his after-lunch pint and chat. The farmer saw him coming, and waited for him. As Dawlish swung into the yard, he grinned.

"In a hurry, Pat?" They were near neighbours and good friends.

"Always in a hurry." Dawlish had his window down, and paused to talk although the minutes were so precious. Marsh might have noticed if anything unusual had happened at Four Ways. Dawlish felt choked. "Don't you ever stay at the farm these days?"

Marsh chuckled.

He was a small man, as men go, broad but thin-hipped. In spite of his ruddy complexion, he didn't really look a farmer. His eyes were too carefree and his manner too casual. An imp of a man, most people thought, and the kind likely to stand for hour after hour with rubber boots right up to his thigh and the trout laughing at him as readily as he laughed at the world. He was a mass of contradictions; the world thought him a bachelor, but in fact he was widowed.

"Oh, I don't keep my nose to the grindstone," he said, "and I don't scorch up the macadam, any time. To see you coming along there you'd think the devil or your wife was on your tail."

"Now would Felicity chase me?" Dawlish felt that chokiness again, but didn't want to raise any alarm—yet. "You wouldn't know if she's home, would you? She often lunches in Haslemere when I'm away, and——"

"Oh, she's home," said Marsh.

"Sure? Don't *shout*."

"I was driving past not an hour ago, and she'd just started out, and then turned back. Saw the car myself. I came straight here and I've seen everything that's passed. If she had, I'd have known. Looked to me as if she'd forgotten something and went back for it."

It was none of Marsh's business to mention Dr. Scott's car. Dawlish found it easier to grin.

"Wouldn't be surprised," he said, "thanks, Bob, I'll go and see how she's getting on. We've friends coming down for the night." He dropped that in casually; the uninvited answer to the questions most likely to spring to Marsh's mind. He felt a hundred times happier, because Marsh had actually seen Felicity out of the house, an hour ago, when he had been approaching Guildford, long after the telephone talk with her. So, she'd not been in such trouble that she couldn't get away.

Had he been fooling himself?

Marsh said: "Well, I'll be going. When are the two of you coming to have a meal with me in a civilized farmhouse?"

"Let's make it soon," said Dawlish. "I'll look in and fix it."

He took the car further into the parking place, and swung it round. The relief was so great that for a few seconds he wanted just to sit there. But not for long. A telephone kiosk stood in a corner of the yard; he could telephone Felicity and put all anxiety behind him within the next two or three minutes.

Why not?

He got out of the car, and then saw another car coming from the direction of Four Ways. It couldn't be coming from anywhere else, to be on that particular road into Alum, it must have come to the crossroads within sight of the house itself. The car was a vivid apple-green Vauxhall, with a youth at the wheel. Dawlish stopped just for a second, to look at him as the car came to a standstill. He was a tall, un-English type with very dark hair, and his hands were firm on the wheel. He hadn't switched off the engine.

The Vauxhall stopped on the other side of the road. Well, why not? Dawlish got out of the Bristol and went to the call-box. He was sharply aware of the other car and the man watching him, told himself that he was dreaming this up, was probably dreaming the whole business up. He squeezed inside the kiosk, but the door wouldn't close properly on his great size. He had his three pennies in his hand, dropped them into the slot and gave his number. Alum 512. Felicity. Home. It was only two miles away, if he'd had any sense he would have gone straight there; Marsh had seen her and she had been all right.

There was no answer.

The operator said: "I'm ringing them for you."

"Thanks."

It wasn't like the *brrr-brrr* of a dialling system telephone, but a series of short, sharp sounds which echoed almost pain-fully in his ear. He was smiling. A few heavy drops of rain fell on the window, but that didn't matter; once he heard Felicity's voice again, thunder and lightning and torrents of rain wouldn't matter.

"I'm still ringing them, if——"

A second voice was superimposed on the operator's; another woman's, but not Felicity's. It was a nice voice. It had the unmistakable tone of an Englishwoman, one associated more with the country and the county than anywhere else.

"Hallo?"

Dawlish said, in flat surprise, "Hallo—is that Alum 512?"

"Yes, it is."

Dawlish's surprise began to ease out. This would be some friend of Felicity's; as often as Felicity went out to lunch, so she had visitors when he was away. This would probably be someone he knew, and who hadn't recognized his voice.

"Is Mrs. Dawlish there?" he asked.

"Well, yes, she is," said the other woman, "but she can't come to the telephone just now, I'm afraid. Who *is* that?"

The tone was one of eager inquiry; she made it sound as if she really wanted to know.

"This is Patrick Dawlish. Do we know each other?" Dawlish asked, and then wished he hadn't; he was very anxious to know why Felicity couldn't come to the telephone. Had she been hurt? This brought a fresh wave of alarm.

"I think we've met at parties," the woman said casually. "But I'm *so* glad you've telephoned—where are you?"

"Alum. What's stopping Felicity from coming to the telephone?"

"It's quite ridiculous," the other woman said, "she slipped and wrenched her ankle, and she's having to lie up. I've put a compress on, and she says it's easier, but—well, I hate to say it, Mr. Dawlish, but I have another engagement and I can't really stay much longer. Could you come right away?"

"Good lord, yes," said Dawlish. "I'm on my way. Have you sent for the doctor?"

There was a pause; then, "Oh, a doctor isn't needed." The emphasis was so great that it puzzled Dawlish, although for the moment that was all. "It's not so very bad, it will be all right when she's rested it for a few hours. You will come right away, won't you?"

"I most certainly will," Dawlish assured her. "I won't be more than five minutes. Good-bye."

He rang off.

As he did so, he glanced across at the Vauxhall, whose driver was undoubtedly watching him. Well, there could be two explanations of that; he might be wanting the telephone, and waiting as patiently as a man could. Or he might be interested in Dawlish.

Stepping out of the box, Dawlish glanced along the row of cottages which comprised most of the High Street of Alum. No one was about; few people ever were at this hour in the afternoon; those who weren't working were sleeping. The end house was Hal Scott's Alum surgery, where he came three times a week to save the older people of Alum the journey into Haslemere. Today was Thursday—one of Hal's mornings. His

Wolseley wasn't there, but it wouldn't take a jiff to go across and leave a message, asking him to come up to Four Ways. Sprained ankles could lead to a lot of trouble.

Dawlish went quickly.

The driver of the Vauxhall didn't get out of the car, but turned his head to watch Dawlish. So the man wasn't after the telephone kiosk.

Dawlish felt his heart beating faster. He couldn't begin to guess why anyone should be so interested in him. Then, nearing Scott's little surgery, he recalled the woman's vehemence. Odd? He was at the little rustic wood gate of the cottage, frowning, when he thought of that. The woman at Four Ways hadn't given her name, had been very casual about whether they had met.

He tapped at the door, and it was opened almost at once by a brisk-looking middle-aged woman, a Mrs. Rapley. She was the wife of one of Marsh's men. Mrs. Rapley was grey, thin, bustling, matter-of-fact and blunt.

"Oh, it's you, Mr. Dawlish," she said, "I was hoping it was the doctor. Where did he go to after calling at your house, can you tell me?" She meant, 'Will you tell me?' "It was his afternoon off, and his wife's been after him three times. I've rung your house but they say he's not there, we just can't find him anywhere."

## CHAPTER X

## FACTS

DAWLISH looked into the woman's thin face and keen grey eyes; and saw her expression change. That could only be because of the look in his eyes. He didn't speak for a moment, and she just waited. He told himself that he must jerk out of this, that he mustn't give Mrs. Rapley cause for alarm and cause for gossip—yet. But it was hard to fight that awful fear —and the fact that he had made a wrong decision.

But Mrs. Rapley wasn't a gossip.

In fact, she could be trusted—if anyone could in Alum Village. That was why she worked for Hal Scott.

Marsh could be trusted, too.

Dawlish made himself relax and speak, and his voice became almost casual.

"That's odd, Mrs. Rapley. I've just come down from London and haven't been home yet, but I'll find out what I can. When did he go up there?"

"Well, it would be about half past eleven," she said. "There was only a small surgery this morning, Mrs. Gittens and her daughter, Old Ben, young—but you won't be interested in that. I made the doctor a cup of tea at eleven o'clock, and then he did some of that paper work that's always driving him to distraction, and then the message came."

"From my wife?"

"Well, yes," said Mrs. Rapley, "but it was very roundabout, really. Seems that Mrs. Dawlish asked the exchange to call the doctor, and they did but they called his surgery in Haslemere. *They* telephoned me. Not that it would take long."

"Do you know why he was wanted?"

"Not a thing more except that it was urgent," said Mrs. Rapley. She raised a hand to her thin neck, and her fingers played nervously. "There isn't any *trouble*, Mr. Dawlish, is there?"

"I'm going home to find out," Dawlish told her, and gave her a smile which set most of her fears at rest. "You don't know where he was going after Four Ways?"

"He said he would look in on old Mrs. Featherstone, on the way back home," Mrs. Rapley told him. "That's about all."

"I'll go and find out where he went to," promised Dawlish, still outwardly confident. "And if there's any news, I'll give you a ring."

"I'd be glad of that," said Mrs. Rapley. "Thank you, sir."

She watched him as he turned away, opening the gate which swung to as he stepped into the street. It was raining; not hard, but just a few heavy spots, and one fell on his eyelid.

He brushed it away. He felt tense and worked up and—frightened because of Felicity. The woman with the pleasant voice and her story of a sprained ankle and the doctor not being called; and the urgent call which had reached Hal Scott—and the fact that Hal hadn't come away.

Face *facts*.

It had sounded odd from the beginning, and now Dawlish knew that there was something gravely wrong. He had to find out what. It was no time, now, to go to the police. Strangers were in possession at Four Ways, and a police raid could lead to disaster; before he did anything he had to find out the true situation. But—what were the probabilities? If it hadn't been for Marsh's reassurance, Dawlish believed that he would be able to see it clearly. Felicity kept at the house. Someone hurt there, badly enough for a doctor to be called—and for the doctor to be held, also. That was it, face *facts*. Hal Scott hadn't had one of his busiest days, and Thursday was always his afternoon off. He wouldn't have stayed a minute longer than was necessary. If anything had been so serious that he needed to stay for so long, at least he would have sent a message.

He hadn't.

So, he *couldn't*. Q.E.D.

By now, Dawlish was back at his car. He didn't appear to notice the man at the wheel of the Vauxhall, although in fact he saw that the man was still there, with his long, pale hands resting on the wheel. The only difference now was that he was smoking. The cigarette was longer than most, and gave him an even more noticeable un-English look.

Dawlish went to The Bull and scribbled a note to Tim Jeremy and Beresford. It told them of trouble with Felicity at the house, and asked them to wait for word from him; they would wait for a while, anyhow.

Then he got into his car.

He started the engine, and then swung round. He took the Four Ways road, which meant passing the Vauxhall. He heard the self-starter scream as he passed. He was thinking of that nice-voiced woman who had told him there was nothing much the matter with Felicity and had urged him to hurry to the house. Of course. If Felicity and Hal Scott were there, then they would expect him, Dawlish, sooner or later; and they would probably prefer it soon.

The raindrops, everything he had heard, the beat of the Bristol's engine and the reflection of the Vauxhall in his driving mirror, all seemed to spell one word—TRAP.

The Vauxhall was coming after him all right.

Something melted in his mind; fear. The heat of a sudden emergency had melted it.

He gave a taut grin, and then put his foot down. The Bristol surged forward with a booming roar. Racing from fifty to eighty in a few seconds, he saw the Vauxhall drop further behind. This was a winding road, especially a little further along, and there were patches of trees; near Four Ways itself, there were tall, thick hedges. He kept his foot down and he kept his wheel over. The danger would come from animals, or from a tradesman's van or a farm cart. So, he hugged the hedges, but he didn't pass a soul, all the way to the cross-roads.

From there, he could see Four Ways.

He judged that he had gained half a mile on the Vauxhall; not far, but enough. He swung his wheel. Tyres screeched as he rounded a corner, then swung close to a hedge and pulled up. The Bristol couldn't be seen from the road along which the Vauxhall was coming.

Dawlish jumped out.

He was at the boot in a flash, flung it up, snatched at the spare wheel. The securing nut was only finger tight. He unscrewed, then heaved the wheel, then lifted it waist high. He carried it into the road along which the Vauxhall would come—along which it was coming fast. He could hear it. Give him time! He dropped the wheel in the middle of the road. A driver's instinctive impulse would be to jam on his brakes, and once the driver of the Vauxhall did that . . .

It came screaming along.

Dawlish backed swiftly behind the hedge, from where he could see without being seen. He heard the car swing round the corner not far along, then heard the first harsh sound of the brakes going on. They didn't squeal, just made the tyres grate on the road surface; and the sound was so loud that Dawlish knew that the natural driving reaction had come. The next would be for the man to sit back if only for a split second, so as to recover from the need for such violent action.

Then he would begin to think.

Dawlish jumped into full view, and ran towards the Vauxhall. It was only ten yards away. The driver was staring at the wheel, sitting back and with his hands raised off the wheel; as if he had been really scared. Of course, he saw Dawlish; but he had very little time to act. He tried to back away, and then tried to get his right hand to his pocket, but that wasn't easy in the restricted space. He had his hand at the flap when Dawlish wrenched open the door. Everything happened with bewildering speed. Dawlish struck him on the side of the face, jolting his head back and making him squeal. His hand came out of his pocket, and something grey showed for a moment, then slipped back.

Dawlish hit him again.

He sensed that the man had lost consciousness, then took the 'thing' out of the big pocket. It was an automatic pistol. Dawlish looked at it for a few seconds—long enough to grapple with the ugly new fact—that an armed man had been waiting to shadow him back to Four Ways.

Dawlish didn't take long to reason that 'they' had probably put someone on the other road, too.

He slid the gun into his pocket, then went to the wheel, raised and wheeled it into the hedge. By the time he had finished, the driver of the Vauxhall was stirring. He was slender, he looked tall, he had sharp features and a rather boyish appearance. His hair was black and glistening with pomade. There was a strong smell of Turkish tobacco in the car.

Dawlish waited.

He could see the roof of Four Ways, and the top of the windows of the ground floor. No smoke was rising. He knew that the coal fires were not usually lit until after lunch, but then there were usually two. He could just see the top of the garage, too, but that was all.

It wouldn't take long to get nearer.

He heard another car . . .

It was coming towards him from the other side of Four Ways; from the way he would have come had he not gone to Alum first. He clipped the Vauxhall driver beneath the jaw again, and sent him back into the coma of unconsciousness, and stepped forward. He could see along that road from the corner; he could even see the approach to Four Ways, although the iron gates weren't visible from here.

The car was much nearer.

He saw it, just the other side of the entrance to the house. It was Felicity's Californian, and was moving fast, but he could see the dented wing, front and bumper. The driver was a man with a fat moon of a face, who had the car very close to the hedge opposite the gates. As Dawlish saw him, he swung the wheel. Brakes groaned. The Californian swung off the road into the drive of the house, and as it disappeared, the driver crashed his gears. The grating sound came high and harsh—and then the motor turned over smoothly in a lower gear, and the car shot up the steep drive towards the house.

Dawlish was a hundred yards away.

He turned, and hurried back to the Vauxhall. He now felt sure of what had happened; his attack on the Vauxhall's driver had been seen by the man in the other car, who had driven back swiftly to Four Ways, to report and raise the alarm.

To whom?

Here was a complete stranger driving Felicity's car, too, and might have been at the wheel when Marsh had seen it. Never mind Marsh. The driver of the Vauxhall was coming round again, his eyes flickering and his mouth working.

Dawlish pushed him to the other side of the car, got in, finding his great legs confined by the dash, started the engine and drove round the corner. He passed the Bristol. Just beyond it was a wide stretch of road, where he could turn. He swung the car round, and finished up half-way on a grass verge, half-way on the road. As he stopped, he felt something sticky on his hand, and glanced down at it involuntarily. The thumb and forefinger with which he had manipulated the gear lever were smeared with red. He looked intently at the lever, and saw a red stain, as well as a brown one; both were sticky.

There were brown spots on the carpet, too.

Blood.

It wasn't any use blinking at facts.

By then, the thin man had started to look about him, and was now staring at him from frightened eyes. A scared, pasty-looking character, who was pressing against his door, as if to keep as far away as he could from Dawlish's fist.

Blood, remember. . . .

But talk of that could wait; fear of what it might mean must wait, too.

Dawlish said softly, slowly: "What you've had is just a taste. If you give me any trouble, I'll break every bone in your body. Understand?"

The man nodded, suddenly, vigorously; and was obviously quite prepared to believe the threat.

"Don't forget it and just answer my questions," Dawlish went on, in the same soft, slow voice. "Is my wife at the house?"

"Ye-es." The one word came out on a high-pitched note, which was probably more due to fear than to the man's natural *timbre*.

"Is she hurt?"

"No!"

"If I find out that she's hurt, I'll——" began Dawlish, but the man didn't let him finish, just raised his hands as if to fend Dawlish off, and insisted in the same high-pitched voice:

"She is not hurt much, just a little wound in the arm, just a *little* one."

Dawlish clenched his teeth.

It would be easy to let himself go, as easy to spend time on the smaller things, the inessentials. He was facing facts, remember. Felicity was a prisoner in their own home. She was hurt, and he could only pray that she wasn't badly injured; certainly he couldn't be sure.

He said, "Is Dr. Scott there?"

"There is the doctor, yes, he—yes!" The thin man eased his collar, although it seemed too large already. His frightened eyes were a browny kind of grey. His complexion was more sallow than olive, and Dawlish placed him as a European from the Balkans. He was fighting his own taut nerves, and putting up a reasonable show.

It would be easy to break his resistance, but the first charge was Felicity. Nothing else mattered; just Felicity and all their future. Whatever he had done wrong already today, he must do the right thing now.

He said:

"Who was hurt in this car?"

The man, who was Webber, flinched.

"*Who was hurt?* If my wife——"

"No, no, it wasn't your wife," Webber cried. "It was—it was a man who—who we wished to stop."

"You and who else? How many of you are at the house?"

"Seven—seven in all," Webber said, hoarsely. "And I, also."

That might be the truth; it sounded plausible. Seven; this man, and Hal Scott and Felicity. What was it all about? He had to find out a little; until he understood what had driven them there he wouldn't know what to do. Minutes were flying, but minutes were less important than making the right decision now.

"Why are your friends there?" he demanded. "What are they doing?"

For the first time, Webber turned away. Rain was falling more heavily now, and spattering the roof of the car; Dawlish heard it rat-tat-tat-ing while he looked at the man's profile, the long, hooked nose, the delicate thin lips.

"Listen," Dawlish said, "I can break your neck as easily as I can snap my fingers." He snapped his fingers, and the noise was sharp and loud. "And if you drive me to it, I will. What are you doing at the house?"

Webber turned to look at him again.

"It was—it was the fault of Prince Josef. Prince Josef himself. He—he was coming to see you because he wanted help. We followed him here, and he was hurt so he had to be—had to be kept here. The doctor was needed also. And—and there is your wife." Webber gulped, as if the sight of Dawlish's expression made his mouth dry. "She—she will not give to Otto the papers which Prince Josef gave to her. That is all," he went on, and his voice was still shrill, his manner more frightened. "There is nothing more I tell you except—except one thing."

He stopped.

The 'prince' sounded almost too unreal to be true, but it wasn't important. The other thing this man could tell him might be.

Dawlish said, in a softer voice even than before, "Before we go on—Prince Josef of where?"

"But of Goetz, of course!"

It meant little; very little—and it didn't affect the real issue. Now, Dawlish asked very gently, "Well, what is that one thing more you can tell me?"


CHAPTER XI

TERMS

THE frightened young man in the Vauxhall did not answer Dawlish at once. The rain came down more sharply, and the windscreen was almost covered, so they saw everything as in a blur. There was no sound but their breathing and the rain. Hours might pass without traffic along here, except at week-ends, when the roads to Surrey's commons and hills were freely used.

Dawlish didn't speak again.

Some new element was frightening this man, and it could only be the fear of telling of the 'one thing'. He couldn't guess how Dawlish would react, he was afraid of an eruption; and by his hesitation, he brought Dawlish's to a simmering point with an eruption only a few seconds away.

He took the bony right wrist.

He didn't twist, just pressed with his great fingers, tightening the pressure slowly and remorselessly; and no vice could have gripped more tightly. Thumb and forefinger were pressed against the sinews and the bone, until the thin man began to sweat and to gasp, and then to shout:

"Stop, I beg you, stop! I will tell you!"

"Go on," said Dawlish, and didn't slacken his grip. "And hurry."

"You are not to take anyone else there, you are not to tell others, not the police, no one! If you do—they will kill your wife, the doctor, *themselves*."

It might be just a threat.

Until that last word came out explosively, that was what it seemed to be, just a threat, the kind that had been uttered a thousand times before and would be again and again. Keep away from the police, *or* . . .

This was different.

It made Dawlish feel better, too; glad that he had played this his own way. If the men had the house and would commit *hara-kiri* . . .

Dawlish put that out of his mind. He stared into the peculiar browny-grey eyes, the quivering lips and the pallid face and believed he was hearing the truth. "If you do—they will kill your wife, the doctor, *themselves*." The last word was the one which made it seem more horrible than anything else, robbed Dawlish of all the ordinary arguments, all the counter-threats, even the dispassionate assessment that was needed.

"They won't kill anyone," Dawlish said roughly. "They'd never get away from the house, they wouldn't stand a chance."

"If they cannot get away," Webber said, "they will kill themselves. They are sworn to do so."

He said that very slowly.

Horror fell upon the air. The wind, blowing down on the car suddenly, seemed to screech a weird accompaniment. This man meant exactly what he said. They would kill themselves rather than allow themselves to be captured, because they were sworn to it.

What hellish thing had happened to send these men here when Felicity had been on her own? What drove them? Who was this Prince Josef? What were the papers which Felicity was said to have? All the questions came swiftly, each forcing the last out, but it was a kind of evasion, a kind of refusal to face the vital fact—that if this man was right the battle was not against ordinary criminals, with whom he might bargain and possibly come to terms, but against fanatics.

Somewhere, vaguely, he seemed to have heard of Prince Josef of Goetz, an obscure Balkan prince who had been in the news. He didn't remember where. He didn't want to think about it, he wanted just to see what he could do to ease the tension of what he had been told.

He said flatly:

"What do they want?"

"It—it would have been no trouble if you had come to the house," the thin man said, with a sudden burst of eagerness. "If you had come you would have been caught, also, and you would have been compelled to stay there for today, perhaps tomorrow, until we could arrange to move the prince. That is all that is required, time for the prince to recover a little and then to be taken away. That is *everything*."

Dawlish said heavily, "Is it?"

"What more should there be?"

Dawlish did not answer.

He could still go for the police, and they would surround Four Ways and then approach it steadily. If there was serious opposition, then they would send for the military; there were several camps nearby. The group of desperadoes in Four Ways could not last for an hour. A whole company of men couldn't hold out for long, there were too many ways of approaching the house. Raiding it and taking possession raised no difficulty, but—how far could this man be believed? Would 'they' rather be killed than caught and, in a kind of valedictory vengeance, would they also kill Felicity?

The risk was there.

Webber went on quickly, eagerly: "That is all they need, I assure you, they need time! *We* need time, for I am one of them, I know all about them. Otto, our leader, is sure that Mrs. Dawlish has these papers. But they will be easy to find; she cannot have hidden them very far, for the prince did not give them to her until this morning. And we need time for His Highness to rest! When he can be taken away, then we shall all go and no one will be hurt." Webber thrust his face closer to Dawlish's, and there was sweat on his long upper lip and on his forehead. "All we need is time why do you not come and see your wife? You will find that she is not badly hurt. There will be no more trouble, until we are gone. It is—it is very *simple.*"

It could work out like that. These men might have got themselves into a corner, and be desperate enough to die rather than be caught; but if they were able to escape, then they might leave nothing but wounded Felicity and Scott behind them.

"If you go alone, all will be well," Webber pleaded. "If you stay here, if you send for the police——" He broke off, and now he actually touched Dawlish's hand. "I know Otto, he will not allow His Highness to be caught, or himself, or Emil."

He did not mention the woman, Hanna.

Dawlish sat there, trying to make up his mind. His teeth were clamped together, and his muscles were stiff, cramped, twitching. There was still so much he didn't know. He had learned a great deal while sitting here with this man, but he didn't know the wider issues. He'd been here for twenty minutes; how much could he learn if he kept the man for as long again? And how much time could he afford to spend on this?

How *badly* was Felicity hurt?

If he submitted, just to help her, would he in fact be helping anyone?

.        .        .        .        .

Felicity was in her bedroom.

After Emil had come running to her, shouting and threatening, she had been allowed to go into the bedroom, and had locked the door. It was a flimsy kind of protection. She could have gone to the window and tried to climb out, but that did not seriously occur to her. There was the telephone, but it was only an extension, and wasn't switched through to the bedroom. She knew that they would watch from the other windows, and she would be seen. She had hardly the strength to move across the room, anyhow. Her arm was aching, and there was a burning sensation in the centre of the wound, too. Her head ached so much that at times it seemed to be lifted off her shoulders. For ten minutes she had sat there with her eyes closed and her head going up and down, aware of hurried movements, men running, car engines starting up, but in such pain that she could pay no real attention.

Her head was a little better, now.

She knew, from what had been shouted to and fro after Emil had rushed up to her, that these men had others to serve them. Two of these men had been watching the Carilon Club, and had known exactly when Dawlish had left. Apparently, the youth once tried to see Dawlish at the club, but had been followed and prevented. Seeing Dawlish's hurried departure, and knowing that he had been due to stay in London all day, they had guessed where he was coming. When the man Webber had telephoned these men from Guildford, where he and the woman Hanna had been, he had been told about Dawlish's departure.

So he had warned Otto and Emil what to expect. There was another thing which would have startled her at any other time; they had talked of His Highness and the prince.

The youth?

Felicity had opened her eyes in time to see the two cars leave: hers had turned towards the stretch of common land towards Guildford, the Vauxhall had gone towards Alum. Whichever way he came, Pat would be intercepted. Felicity had known the simple, terrifying truth: that they had gone to watch for Pat, and to trap him, and there was nothing at all that she could do to stop it.

Then, she had seen the Californian come back, driven at wild speed.

She'd heard the squeal of brakes at the crossroads, too—drivers who didn't know the spot often came too fast, and in order to get round the corner safely, jammed on their brakes. But this had taken on a new significance, for the unwary driver might be Pat.

He wouldn't be unwary, though; he would be warned.

The Vauxhall hadn't come back.

The silence that had fallen after the bustle, had lasted for nearly half an hour. Now and again she heard a man speak, but that was all.

Pat still hadn't arrived, then; just hadn't come.

Did he know for certain what had happened, now? When he did, what would he do? Would he come, driving or walking, simply to share her plight? Or would he find a way of fighting?

She heard a man speaking again, but didn't strain her ears to listen, because there was no way in which she could hear, unless she went downstairs. So, she sat here. The rain, falling very fast, was streaming down the window. The sky was a uniform dark grey, everywhere. It was half-past two, and almost as dark as night.

A *night* here.

She wondered how the youth was.

She wondered how Hal Scott was.

∙　　∙　　∙　　∙　　∙

Dr. Hal Scott ran his hands over his face, felt the rasp of stubble, for he was a twice-a-day shaver, moistened his lips, and then turned away from the window and looked into the teeming rain. He could see the man in the little summer-house, watching the window here, and placed so that he could see anyone who came from the house at this side or the front; and anyone who approached from the drive or from the gate in the wall on the far side of the drive. This man had been cleverly placed; anyone with less experience of putting out guards would have needed two or three to do the work of this one.

Nothing had moved, except the trees and bushes in the wind, since Felicity's smashed car had come up the drive, driven at speed by the fat brute. He had come storming in, and for a few minutes afterwards, Scott had expected a summons; but none had come.

He turned away and went to the boy who still lay on that improvised bench.

The pale face with the dark hair and the dark curling lashes looked like the face of death, but this youth wasn't dead. He wasn't likely to die, either. He could die, if he was left long enough without the proper attention, but he would come through all right even if he had no better nursing than they could give him here. Scott had tried hard to make the others believe that the youth was at the point of death; he didn't think he had failed, but believed that rather than allow themselves to be caught, they would let 'His Highness' die.

Scott stared at that young face.

Was it vaguely familiar? Had he seen the youth before, either in the flesh or in a photograph? Or had he seen him so much in the past hour or so that the face was impressed upon his mind's eye so that it seemed like an old picture?

Scott simply didn't know.

He moved sharply, away from the wounded youth towards the door. He didn't know whether it was locked. He had stayed here with his charge, fighting against the impulse to do what Felicity had done, and try to escape. If he once let himself go, he might run amok. He knew himself only too well. Once let his temper flare and . . .

If he judged them aright, they would shoot him down.

*If* he judged them aright . . .

There were moments when he argued with himself that they wanted to save the life of 'His Highness' and, if he tried to escape and they brought him back, they would not kill him because they would want him to look after the youth. There was no real certainty of that, but there was of one thing. If he once escaped, he wouldn't let them catch him again. He would fight while he had any breath left, he would never be able to control and calm himself.

It was hard enough, now.

How would it help if he let go? There was the youth and there was Felicity, as well as he himself.

But he couldn't stay here!

He felt like bellowing that as he reached the door and turned the handle. He had to get out, he couldn't breathe in this room, he would burst.

He . . .

The door opened, and he had pulled so savagely that it banged against his knee. He winced, and backed away, then rubbed his knee and felt foolish. He even grinned. The passage was empty, no one stood on guard, and they hadn't even troubled to lock the door. That gave him an idea of how seriously they worried about him.

He heard voices.

He tried the door which led to the kitchen quarters, but that was locked; and Dawlish was a believer in strong mortice locks. An expert cracksman might be able to force one, but that wasn't his *forte*. The voices were coming from the front room, and the door was open.

He crept along, making little sound, but fearful of his shoes squeaking on the parquet floor.

Part of the time, the men talked in a language which Scott didn't understand, but whenever the girl was present, they talked in French, and Scott was almost as fluent in French as in his mother tongue.

He heard the name 'Dawlish'.

He drew nearer.

He heard Otto say in his precise but rather tired voice:

"Hanna, do we need to say this again and again? It is not the situation that we desired, but it has happened now and there is nothing we can do. We did not want Josef to come here. We tried to keep him away from Dawlish, but—he came, and we were unable to stop him. It is unfortunate, but we must face the situation. Now that he has adopted such an attitude, would it be better for our country if he was dead?"

Hanna seemed to catch her breath.

"You must not be sentimental," Otto chided; and that was exactly the tone of his voice—*chiding*. "He was the figurehead, but now—that is over. We keep him alive now because we want to find out who has the documents, if he did not bring them here. He is known to have tried to see Dawlish in London, so it is possible that he gave them to Dawlish, or sent them to him. He——"

"Would he part with them to a stranger?" That was Emil.

"In his distress, it is possible that he would," said Otto, quietly. "Or, he has put them somewhere safe. It was clever of him to have a set of false documents, with which to deceive us. However—the real ones might be here, Mrs. Dawlish might have a good hiding-place. Or, when he comes, Dawlish might know where they are, but until we are sure, we need the prince alive."

"We also want to know who else he has talked to and who knows he is in England," Hanna said, very quietly. "Dawlish may know——"

"That is so. If no one, it is good. If——"

"There is one thing you appear to forget," said Hanna, in a different voice.

"What is that?"

"Will Dawlish come by himself, or will he bring the police?"

After a pause, Otto said quietly:

"If he comes alone, it is good. If he brings others, then the time has come for us all to die."

He stopped, but only for a moment; and his voice grew brisker. "If others know the prince is here the damage is done, but"—it was possible to imagine him shrugging his square shoulders—"how can we be sure of that? We simply cannot allow it to become known that Prince Josef is here. So, how can we allow anyone who has seen us to talk—to the police, the newspapers, and so to the world? No, it is most unfortunate but we cannot allow anyone who has seen us to remain alive, and be a constant threat to all our hopes. Even *you* will agree to that."

The girl didn't speak.

Emil said smoothly: "Of course she agrees, Otto. That is
not our anxiety. Our anxiety is Dawlish himself, and Webber.
What will Dawlish do? If he comes alone, good, if not—well,
we know what to do, but I prefer to live. And—what will
Webber say to Dawlish? Can he even be trusted? All we know,"
he added, in the same smooth voice, "is that Dawlish and
Webber are still at the crossroads, and Dawlish has not yet
left. Shall I tell you what I think?"

No one spoke.

"I will tell you what I think," Emil went on, and there
was an unmistakable edge of cruelty in his voice. "It is time
that we went to see this Dawlish. *I* will go. I shall tell him that
I come to parley with him, and when I am close enough to be
sure, I shall shoot him. We must get him away from that
position soon and we need Webber. Is that not true?"

There was another silence.

"Yes," Otto said at last, "it is true. Hanna, I dislike the
need for this just as much as you, but Emil is right. If Dawlish
will not come to us, then we must go to Dawlish. We must
find out what is known."

"Now," insisted Emil.

Otto said, "Yes, now."

.     .     .     .     .

Hal Scott heard every word of that.

It was a measure of the contempt in which they held him
that they had not locked him in; and had not troubled to make
sure that he couldn't overhear. They would believe him safely
confined, sure that the guards would stop him if he made a
bid to escape, but—their contempt didn't matter. His life,
Felicity's and now Dawlish's were at the mercy of this group,
and only he was aware of it.

He knew exactly what he had to do.

Warn Dawlish.

CHAPTER XII

## WARN DAWLISH

HAL SCOTT moved swiftly away from the hall, along the passage, and to the unlocked door. No one saw him. He did not wait for Emil to come into the hall, but slipped into the morning-room and closed the door. As he pushed it to, he held his breath, fearful in case it should click and so warn Emil.

It made no sound.

Nor did Prince Josef.

Scott glanced at the youth but hardly gave him a thought; there would be time for that later if he could get out and tell Dawlish. If? He *must*. He didn't think beyond that, and the conviction that these men would do exactly what they threatened if they were not baulked.

He picked up a small pair of pincer-tongs from the fire-place, and a short poker, both of brass. He slipped these beneath his coat, buttoned his coat tightly, then looked out of the window. He saw the man in the summer-house. This guard would turn this way at the slightest sound.

This wasn't the way to go.

Scott opened the door again, and listened. He heard Emil, still talking. He went out. The kitchen door locked him out effectively, but there was the staircase and the upper rooms. In a downstairs room he might be interrupted at any moment. From upstairs, the risk of being seen from the grounds was greater, but—he had to take one chance or the other. He stepped boldly into the hall. If it came to a point, he would have to run for it; the sound of shooting would reach Dawlish if he was at the crossroads; and they wouldn't make a mistake about that.

Emil was actually standing in the doorway of the drawing-room, listening to Otto. Otto was giving him precise instructions, and Emil shuffled his feet, as if impatient. Scott reached the foot of the stairs. If he could reach the half landing, he would have won a good start. But if Emil turned round . . .

Scott went up the stairs.

The carpet muffled the sound of his footsteps. He was breathing hard when he reached the landing, but didn't wait to make sure whether he had escaped unseen. He crossed to the main spare room, hesitated, and then turned along a narrow passage towards the small but pleasant rooms which were kept for the living-in staff. Now, there was only Maude; lucky Maude.

This room overlooked the orchards at the side of the house.

A man stood, motionless, near the wall, but there would be one wherever Scott made his attempt. This man could see the side and back of the house, and the whole stretch of the drive on this side. The acute danger came from him, but this was the best side to try, for Scott was out of sight of the front of the house, and it would take longer for Otto or the other guard to come to this man's help.

Scott opened a window.

The guard didn't look round.

Scott looked down. The window was immediately above the roof of the back porch. If he could get to that and then jump and land on grass the dull thud might reach the guard's ears, but he might be lucky. There was a beech hedge, behind which he could crouch out of sight. It was touch and go, now, and Scott felt his breath coming in panting gasps. It didn't occur to him to back out; he simply had no choice.

He climbed out of the window.

For a moment, he stood in the beating rain, swaying. It was the hiss of rain which had saved him, so far—that, and the fact that the guard's duty was obviously to make sure that no one came in, rather than to see that no one got out. He did not once look round.

The rain came, hissing; the wind blew a flurry of dead leaves, adding to the noise which was blessed in Scott's ears. He went down on all fours, and reached the edge of the roof.

The jump was a long one—so long that there was a real danger that he would make so much noise that the guard couldn't fail to hear him.

He turned round, so that his back was towards the guard; and that was his worst moment, so far; he couldn't be sure whether he was watched or not. He didn't look round, but lowered himself gradually, scraping his knee on the sharp guttering, and clenched his teeth against the pain. He didn't make any more sound than the rain. The guttering was half full of water, and he splashed into this; some ran down his sleeve and he shivered; but he didn't hesitate and didn't let go. He lowered himself over the roof until he was hanging at full length. If the guard turned and saw him now, it would be like shooting at a sitting bird. And this man would be able to shoot; Scott didn't fool himself about that.

He dropped.

The gravel of the drive was hard and loose. He made so much noise that he was sure he must be heard. He turned and leapt for the cover of the hedge, diving full length on to the grass. He slithered over it, and his grazed knee stung like fury, but he didn't cry out. He could no longer see the guard, but would know if the man were coming this way. He raised his head, slowly and fearfully, towards the top of the hedge. There was a tiny gap through which he might be able to see without being seen. A row of smooth stones, heavy and easy to throw, ran along by the hedge. Scott picked one up, and clutched it.

The guard was staring intently towards the house.

And—Scott had left the window open.

He saw the man clearly, short and lean, wearing a rain-coat and a wide-brimmed hat, off which the rain dripped a little. He had an automatic in his hand, cocked and pointing towards the house. He looked right and left first, and then his gaze lifted towards the window through which Hal Scott had climbed.

His mouth opened.

Scott saw that, and jumped up, still clutching one of the stones. In the split second that followed, he caught the man by

surprise, forcing a momentary hesitation; then he hurled the
stone. As he did so, the man fired.

The crack was sharp and clear; the flash bright against
the gloom.

Scott leapt.

He felt the bullet pluck into his right shoulder, and it swung
him round. He saw, like a picture a long way off, the stone
strike the guard on the face, just below the eye, and he saw the
man stagger. He didn't fall, himself, but staggered helplessly for
several seconds; but the guard fell, with the gun in his hand.

If only he hadn't fired. . . .

Scott gritted his teeth, and made himself move forward.
The guard lay still. With that gun, Scott thought, he was as
good as free. With that gun he could fight his way to Dawlish.
Scott had recovered from the force of the blow. His shoulder
felt numbed, and it would soon start to hurt. That didn't
matter, it needn't put him out of action.

He wrested the gun from the guard's limp hand.

He brought the butt down, fiercely, on to the man's
temple and prayed that he wouldn't have to worry about him
for a long time; time enough for this gamble to be finished one
way or the other.

He turned towards the drive, and began to run.

If he could get a chance to shoot the other guard, he
would have a clear run.

No, wait. Emil would be going that way, on his treacherous
errand. Would it be better to go through the gate in the wall,
run along the meadow to the road and then along the road?
He actually started out for the gate, when he realized that if he
did it that way he would give the others time to get to the
end of the drive and lie in wait for him.

He had to shoot his way through.

No one was about; no one seemed to have heard the
shot. That wasn't reasonable. They'd heard, and were lying
in wait. He glanced up at the top windows of the house, and
then he saw Felicity. She stood at a window, her face white
with fear, and was trying desperately to get the window open.
She seemed to be shouting.

A warning?

The window crashed open, and Felicity's voice was suddenly loud against the rain and the wind.

"Hal, they're coming for you. *Run!*"

She could see from windows on either side, and would know exactly what was happening. Scott turned and ran towards the little gate in the wall. That was his only chance, after all —and as he reached the grass banks at the side of the drive he told himself that it might be better to try and get to Marsh at Alum Farm. Marsh would come to help, and he wouldn't have to double back and risk running into an ambush.

His shoulder began to ache.

His arm was wet and sticky, and the blood had reached his wrist and his hand.

"*Hal!*" screamed Felicity.

She was still at the window, when Scott looked round. The other guard was near the bank, and Emil was there, too. Scott fired, twice, didn't wait to see whether he had scored a hit, but turned and ran towards the gate in the wall. Once he could get behind that wall there was some kind of cover, he would have a chance of a kind.

It was only three yards away.

He heard the shots ring out. They weren't very loud; it was a crackling kind of sound. He felt a bullet bite into his waist, on one side, and another into his right shoulder; it couldn't be more than an inch or two from the first wound, and it nearly spun him round. Trees, bushes, the rain, the leaden skies, the house itself, Felicity standing at the window, and the two men who were chasing him seemed to spin round and round; and they wouldn't stop. Scott didn't know that he was still running mechanically, his legs were working at some subconscious order from his mind. He reached the gate. He didn't turn round again. There was pain at his waist and at his shoulder, but he mustn't let anything stop him.

He reached the meadow and turned left, towards the road. He was gasping for breath. He didn't really hope that he would be able to get to Dawlish, now, but felt simply that he must go on, he couldn't go back. On, on, on, as far and as fast as his legs would take him. They seemed to be folding up. He wasn't so much running as staggering, with his arm drooping and when he nearly fell his hands actually touched the tufts of grass.

Then, he saw someone not far along the wall, and he could hardly believe his eyes. It was like a dream. But a man was coming towards him, running fast. It was Bob Marsh, of Alum Farm. He was carrying something; a gun, a *shot*gun? He wasn't more than thirty or forty yards away, coming to his, Scott's, help. But it wasn't he, Scott, who needed help, It was Dawlish who needed warning.

Scott heard another sharp crack of a shot.

He didn't feel anything, and didn't attempt to look behind. He saw Marsh put his gun to his shoulder, heard the roar of the shot, and then pitched forward. For a few seconds he didn't know anything, except the confusion of sounds and thoughts in his head, and the pain at his waist and his shoulder. Then he felt hands touch him, and heard Marsh saying:

"Hal, what are they doing? What devilry——"

Scott gasped: "Daw-Daw-Dawlish at cross-cross-cross-roads. Warn him c-c-coming to talk, they'll shoo-shoo-shoo-shoot him. Warn Dawlish, warn——"

Another crack of a shot came screaming.

.        .        .        .        .

Bob Marsh, tramping across the meadow because it was a short cut to a spinney on the other side of the road where he could pick up a few rabbits and do a few kitchens and his own corn some good, had his .22 tucked under his arm, his gaiters and heavy boots on, and his old tweed hat on the back of his head. There were few happier men than Marsh, and he was thinking of Dawlish and his pleasant wife and his reputation, when he heard the sound of a shot. Would that be Dawlish? He couldn't think of anyone else who would be shooting near here, but it didn't sound like a small-bore.

By then, Marsh was near the road.

Next, he heard shouting; and what sounded like a woman

screaming. He turned and stared back, but could only see the roof of Four Ways. He began to run. He was half-way along when Scott appeared, and he didn't need telling that Scott was badly injured.

Then, a man appeared at the gate.

Scott pitched forward almost at that moment, and the man at the gate had his gun poised. Marsh threw himself to one side, raising his small bore as he did so. After one shot, he saw the man at the gate duck; for a moment there was silence except for Scott's awful breathing.

Silence. . . .

But at Four Ways there was Felicity Dawlish. Here was a badly wounded man. And there was Scott's almost incoherent message, which could only mean one thing.

Dawlish was at the crossroads, and in danger of being trapped.

Armed men had possession of Four Ways.

Marsh had to decide whether to leave Scott here, perhaps to die; whether to try to help Felicity Dawlish; or whether to turn and run towards the road and hope that he could reach Dawlish in time to give him the warning.

Then . . .

That didn't matter.

He heard a different sound; a kind of gasp from Scott, at which his body heaved; and then a rattle as from his throat, and collapse to stillness.

Now he felt sure that Scott was dead.

He knew a moment of shocked horror.

He stared towards the gate, and a bullet struck a stone not a foot away from him; chippings stung his cheek. Someone appeared for a split second, gun levelled, and Marsh ducked low and then turned and, bent almost double, made for the road.

## CHAPTER XIII

# WARNING

DAWLISH heard the shooting.

The man Webber also heard it, and raised his head sharply, looking towards Four Ways. A gust of wind came howling at them, and it was impossible to judge whether there were more shots or not. There was a lull in the wind but not in the hissing rain, and Dawlish tried to hear more distant sounds, but could not.

He didn't speak; but he knew exactly what he had to do.

He turned in the car, and rammed a fist against Webber's chin, jolting the man into unconsciousness. From then on he moved at bewildering speed. His face didn't change expression and it showed no sign of alarm; in fact, he looked more like a statue carved out of wood than a man. He pushed Webber towards the open door on the passenger's side, then got out, went round, picked the man up bodily and carried him to the back of the car.

The boot wasn't locked.

He pushed Webber into it, laying him on his back with his legs doubled up, and locked the boot. He dropped the keys into his pocket, then turned and ran towards the Bristol. He was at the wheel in a few seconds, ripped her into gear and to life, and shot off towards Four Ways. The roaring drowned every other sound, but that didn't matter. There was Felicity and shooting and he hadn't a thought in his mind except getting to the house.

He roared towards the drive.

He actually swung his wheel, to turn into the drive, when he saw someone burst into the road, a little way along, and then come running. He didn't recognize the man at first, but stopped the car and snatched out the stolen gun in the same split second.

Then he recognized Marsh.

Marsh looked up, saw him, and waved desperately. Dawlish was at the end of the drive and, leaning forward, could just see the house itself. He got out. Marsh waved wildly again, as if warning him to get inside, but Dawlish edged towards the drive gate.

He saw a big, fattish man, hurrying into Four Ways. The Californian was parked near the open front door. There was no sign of anyone else.

Marsh came, gasping, almost in a state of collapse.

Dawlish grabbed, and stopped him from falling, but couldn't stop the farmer from dropping his gun. It clattered on the wet tarmac. Rain streamed down the sides of the road and splashed up knee high.

Marsh was gasping, nearly as incoherent as Scott had been.

"They've killed Scott, *killed* him. He said—he said they're going to trap you, something about a parley, they——" Marsh stopped, gasping desperately for breath, and when he started again he had said almost exactly the same words. The first three registered on Dawlish's mind as if they had been burned in with a branding iron.

*"They've killed Scott."*

Marsh began to speak more clearly, and to stand more upright, leaning against the Bristol, and with a hand pressed into his stomach. He was nearer sixty than fifty, and he had run three hundred yards at desperate pace.

"Saw—saw your wife. She—she was shouting."

"You saw her just *now*?"

"Yes," Marsh said, "she was at a top-floor window, no—no doubt about it. In God's name, Pat, what's happened here? Murder and kidnapping and——"

"Bob," Dawlish said in a stony voice, "I don't know what's happened, but I'm going to find out."

Marsh's face was working as he fought for breath.

"Don't go—don't go walking into that holocaust. They'll murder you. Get the police, get——"

He broke off.

Dawlish said: "Listen, Bob. I don't know much more about it than you do, but Felicity's up there. I've got to get to her.

Understand? And listen. *Listen!*" he roared, and gripped the
farmer's shoulder and shook him. "Stop making that din, and
*listen!*"

Marsh had only been gasping.

"I'm going up there," Dawlish went on in a stony voice.
"You go to the village. *Don't* call the police yet. I want an
hour to see if I can handle this on my own. An hour. Get that?"
His voice roared out.

Marsh raised a clenched fist. "Listen to me, it's suicide!
They'll shoot you as lief as look at you. Don't——"

"Bob," Dawlish made himself say evenly, "I'm going to
Felicity. I want an hour's grace. You get into Alum, and——"

"But Pat, they'll——"

"Keep your ruddy mouth shut and listen to me!" roared
Dawlish, and his great hands clenched Marsh's shoulders and
gripped so tightly that the farmer was shocked into being
absolutely still and silent. Water dropped from the shapeless
brim of his tweed hat, and down his face; water dripped from
Dawlish's corn-coloured hair, his eyelashes, down his cheeks,
under his chin and into his collar. "Now, Bob," Dawlish went
on more calmly, "in an hour I might be able to sort things out.
Perhaps they're a crowd of lunatics, perhaps—never mind.
I want one hour. Two men will be at The Bull, inside that
hour. You've met them. Tim Jeremy and Ted Beresford.
Remember?" That word was barked.

Marsh said, "Yes," in a hopeless kind of voice.

"They'll know what to do. Tell the police if you must, but
make sure I get my hour's grace. If I don't it might make
the difference between life and death." He gripped Marsh's
shoulders even more tightly, and then let him go. "There's a
Vauxhall at the corner. Use it." He took the keys out of his
pocket, and handed them to Marsh—and then he turned
towards the Bristol. "There's a chap in the boot, he might be
able to help."

"In the—*boot*?"

Dawlish said, "That's right."

He opened the door of the Bristol, got in, and slammed it.
Marsh hesitated for a moment; and then, as if realizing the

desperate importance of every second, he broke into a shambling run, head down so that the wind and the rain did not beat into his face. He slithered and splashed. Dawlish saw him in the driving mirror, but didn't look into it for long. He started the engine, and turned the wheel, eased off the brake, and then put the nose of the Bristol towards Four Ways.

The drive seemed empty and desolate.

The rain swept across from the leafless trees and the leafless bushes, ran down the gulleys at either side. The wind bent the saplings and the smaller bushes, and there was a constant movement. As the rain beat down and hissed, so the wind howled. At the top of the drive, on the hill which he had come to love over the years, Four Ways looked solitary and distinguished, a house of mock-Tudor style, strongly built, beautifully placed. Even the storm could not spoil the attractiveness of it.

He couldn't see any sign of movement.

He did see that the front door was open.

He did not see Emil, or three other men, all of them armed, watching and waiting for him.

·    ·    ·    ·    ·

Felicity did not know what had happened to Hal Scott; she could only pray that he had escaped. Hope, pray, and wait in this locked room, before they came for her. There was nothing she could do to keep them out. Since Scott had disappeared on the other side of the wall, one of the guards had taken up his position there. Obviously he had been hurt; she could see the big bruise at his eye, even from here; his eyes seemed to be closed up. Now, he walked to and fro, looking in all directions all the time.

Felicity had closed the window.

There was very little that she understood, but one thing seemed certain: these men would not let her get away from here alive if it was possible to stop her.

She saw a movement of some kind at the foot of the drive, but had no idea what it was; the hedge and the trees were too high. She stood there, staring out, so tense that her finger-nails hurt the palms of her hand—and although she was aware of pain, she didn't unclasp her hands. If Pat was down there, if Pat came here, he would walk into a trap from which there would be no escape.

She knew that another guard was on the other side of the house. She didn't see Emil, standing and waiting just inside the doorway, which stood wide open. She sensed more than knew that it would be deadly for Pat to come here, and as she watched the foot of the drive, she prayed that he would go away. Better one of them should die than both.

She didn't realize how completely empty of hope she had become.

Then, she heard a tap at the door. It was so faint at first that she didn't realize what it was; even the second and the third time it was faint, but she knew where it came from. She turned away from the window, hating the need to. As she crossed the room, she looked behind her—but nothing else had happened at the gates. She didn't know that she might have seen Bob Marsh rush across the opening, to fall into Pat's arms.

*Tap-tap-tap.*

She reached the door. She couldn't begin to guess who was there or who would tap. Not the men, surely, unless . . .

Emil?

Why should he want to enter furtively? If they were ready to question her again, they could force the door with little trouble. It puzzled her, and she hesitated; should she open the door, or call a question, or . . .

The tapping came again, and seemed sharp and urgent.

There was no point in keeping the door locked; not when she faced the issue squarely. If they wanted to open it, they could. She knew that, and yet still hesitated—until, as the tapping started again, she snatched at the key, turned it, opened the door and stood back.

It was the girl, Hanna.

Hanna slipped inside, very quickly, and closed the door. She had a wild look. In the simple grey suit, which suited her, she looked smaller than when Felicity had first seen her; and she also looked scared. Her fair hair was long, ruffled, falling almost to her shoulders. Her eyes were that clear, limpid grey of a mountain stream.

The latch clicked.

She said urgently: "I must talk to you and they mustn't know that I am here." She turned the key in the lock and then moved across the room, but kept away from the window. She turned to look at Felicity. "I want to help you," she said, "but I don't know for certain whether I can. *They* mean to kill you. You've seen Josef and you've seen Otto, and . . ." She shrugged, as if there was nothing more to say; she was silent for what seemed a long time, and then she went on quietly: "If you give him these papers, it might help you. I don't say that it will, but it might."

Then, she stopped.

And then, before Felicity began to understand the full significance of what was happening, a car engine roared at the foot of the drive. Felicity swung round and ran towards the window—and saw Dawlish at the wheel of the Bristol, coming up as if he meant to smash his way into the house.


CHAPTER XIV

## THE ACT OF DAWLISH

FELICITY held her breath as the red car came streaking up. Hanna joined her, no longer keeping away from the window, drawn as by a magnet. She held Felicity's arm tightly, as if she shared her tension. The roar of the engine was like a low-flying aircraft. It shut out all other sound.

The Bristol swallowed up the drive.

To Felicity and the watching girl it seemed that Dawlish was going to crash deliberately; as if he hadn't time to save himself. Felicity knew that couldn't be true, and yet the fear was there. Dawlish himself was out of sight, now; all she could see was the shining top of the Bristol—and it went *swisssh!* out of sight.

How could it fail to crash?

Wheels screamed and the brakes howled. Felicity leaned forward to see everything she could. The Bristol had slewed round, and she guessed that its nose was actually on the porch, blocking all exit from the house this way. She heard a door slam. She knew that Pat hadn't crashed—but there was no time to feel relief, little time even to feel hope. Four armed men were waiting for him, and they had wanted him to come. Now, she held her breath, expecting the sound of shooting and frightened almost to move.

Would they shoot?

Could he save himself?

It didn't really occur to Felicity that he might be able to save her as well.

.     .     .     .     .

Dawlish saw the house looming up as he hurtled towards it. There hadn't been much time to gain speed, but the car was so highly powered that it hardly mattered; and fifty up that drive was like a hundred on the open road. Everything in sight was crystal clear: the house, the leaded panes, the almost gargoyle-like face of a man at one window—and Felicity. He caught only a glimpse of her at her bedroom window, and he knew at least that she was alive.

He exulted.

He kept his foot hard down until it seemed impossible to stop in time. The gargoyle had disappeared. He saw a fat man appear at the front door for an instant, level his gun and fire, and then dart back out of sight. He would be scared; all of them would be.

Dawlish was grinning.

He jammed his foot on the brake, and the car lifted off the ground but didn't skid; the gravel gripped the tyres. It slithered to a standstill, with the front wheels actually touching the porch steps. He was out of it and slamming the door in a trice, with the gun in his hand. He leapt over the nose of the Bristol, which was hot to touch, and landed in the hall. He saw the fat man in a doorway, looking pale and scared—he didn't see the man's gun, but had no doubt that it was there.

He roared, "Come out of it, you skulking addlepates, come and fight it out!" and his voice seemed to boom about the hall, travel up the stairs, shiver into the rooms on either side. He fired at the fat man who darted out of sight again. A bullet struck the floor a few inches from Dawlish's right foot, and he kicked out, as if he wanted to kick it back. He saw the open door of the drawing-room, and the little man with the wrinkled forehead and the wizened face, and loosed a shot at him. The little man skipped, then jumped, as if a jumping cracker was at his heels.

"Anyone here want Patrick Dawlish?" roared Dawlish, and he leapt for the stairs. He didn't know whether anyone was up there, as well as Felicity. All he wanted was to get to her, and nothing was going to stand in his way; but he might have to shoot it out. "Coming, Fel, stay where you are!" he roared, and as he neared the half landing, he glanced over and saw the fat man, crouching at a partly-open door, and pointing his gun upwards.

Dawlish ducked, heard the sharp spitting sound of the shot, and fired at the man. The door slammed, and the bullet buried itself into the wood. But as he took the next step Dawlish saw another man on the other side of the hall, and a levelled automatic.

Dawlish dropped to his knees.

He fired between two banister rails, heard the kind of cry he wanted to hear, and saw his man vanish into an open doorway.

Now, if no one was up here, he would be all right.

He jumped the last three stairs, and reached the main landing. The bedroom door was closed. He looked right and left and saw no one. He heard a slithering sound below, and swayed to one side; the sound was followed by another shot. He flattened himself against a wall, opposite the bedroom, and roared:

"Why don't you come and fight it out, you shivering lumps of blubber? Come and fight, no holds barred. Show your moon faces, you *cretins*, let's see if you walk or crawl."

He stopped.

When the echo died away, there was absolute silence.

Felicity was in that room only a few yards away from him. Once it was open, he could reach it in a bound, but he couldn't go to it yet, because if he had to stop to try to break it down, he would be a standing target for anyone who crept up the stairs; and they would soon be creeping, if they hadn't started already.

Why didn't Felicity open the door?

Why didn't——

A shot spat out, and a bullet struck the door in front of his eyes. It made the wood shiver. A split appeared in a panel at about waist height. He wasn't sure whether it bit its way through, he couldn't be absolutely sure, but if anyone were standing on the other side and a bullet did go through, then a nasty wound——

"Fel!" Dawlish shouted, "stand to one side, don't stand in front of——"

*Crack. Crack-ack-ack-ack-ack.*

The fat man, and perhaps others with him, were standing in the hall and out of Dawlish's sight and range; but they could see the bedroom door, and they were shooting to try to make sure that Felicity couldn't open it. There was no way to stop them. If he went towards the door now, he would run through the hail of bullets; and the moment they saw him move again, they were bound to shoot.

They stopped, making a welcome lull.

Dawlish watched the door—and saw the handle turning, heard the faint sound of it. In a moment, the door would sag open. He didn't know whether Felicity had been hit, only knew that the handle was turning, and that once the door was off the latch, he would leap towards it. He would be in the line of fire for a split second, and provided he kept low he would have a chance to dodge the bullets.

Would he?"

He knew this landing as he knew this house; every piece of furniture, every crack in the ceiling, every chip of plaster and every chip in the paint. He was against the wall next to the bathroom. He could get into the bathroom, and grab something to throw.

What was there in the room?

He found himself grinning. In war and in the violent days of peace he had known of times like this; and now that he felt sure that he was between Felicity and the enemy, he was half-way through the battle. He could afford to allow something to well up in him, to take possession of him; an almost animal delight in his own strength and in a fight for its own sake. This was the quality which had made him hero to so many boys; and a headline in so many newspapers the world over.

If he could be sure that Felicity was in there and not in urgent danger . . .

The door opened a fraction. "Pat," she called, and her voice was crystal clear, and for the moment, free from fear. "Pat, be *careful.*"

He gasped.

"Be *careful——*" she repeated.

He exploded into a bellow of laughter which must have shaken the men below as much as a fusillade of bullets. Felicity could go through all this, hear the shooting, feel that the next might be her own or his last moment, and she could say as she might when he was taking the Bristol out for a spin, "Pat, be *careful.*"

He called, with the laughter still in his voice:

"Stay where you are, I'm coming."

He sidled towards the bathroom door, and took off his coat as he did so. He held the coat up by the collar and tossed it across the landing. The men were fooled, as he had hoped they would be; the shots rattled out, smacking into the door and pushing it wider. As the shooting came, so Dawlish dived into the bathroom, collected the stool, glasses from the shelf and two bottles which stood by the side of the bath; disinfectants and a detergent. The shooting had stopped when he reached the landing again; he knew that they were puzzled, and were waiting. He stretched up and took an electric light bulb out of a lamp socket, and tossed it over the banisters as joyously as he would a Mills bomb.

It struck the floor, and burst with almost as much noise.

He flung the bathroom stool, the glasses and then the bottles into the hall, and as the last fell, he dived across towards the door. He reached it with his hands and thrust it open and wriggled inside. Felicity was standing just behind the door; and behind her was another girl. He didn't spare either of them more than a glance, but sprang to his feet and slammed the door, then turned the key in the lock. He heard the muffled crack of a shot, and saw a bullet break the wood of the door and fall half-way across the room.

He grinned brightly.

"Hallo," he greeted. "Sorry I'm late, especially as we've company." He stretched out a great arm and gave his Felicity a bear-hug—but he missed her injured arm. Next, he beamed at Hanna and then went on in exactly the same tone, "Keep where you are, I won't be a jiff." He strode across the room to one of the twin beds, gripped and dragged it and then pushed it against the door. He went for the other bed and stood this on its end so that the top rested on the door and the bottom on the floor. Then he put all his weight against it, jamming it as tightly as he could. Next, he pulled, but didn't shift it far; it made a good barricade.

"No tame Hercules down there, is there?" he asked the other girl; and then he appeared to see her properly for the first time. "*My!*" he breathed, "I'm really beginning to live."

Hanna looked at him, then towards Felicity; and her expression seemed to plead, "What do I say; is he always like this?" Dawlish grinned, took out cigarettes, and proffered them. Hanna took one eagerly. He lit it for her, and let the lighter flame burn. He appeared only to be thinking about the cigarettes, and drew in deeply, holding his head back a little. In fact, he was listening; and what was more, he was moving slowly towards the window as he did so. He didn't go close to it, but kept to one side. He looked out into the grounds, and saw no one.

"They may try to get in this way," he remarked, reasoningly. "More likely to wait until after dark, though—unless they decide that this is the end and they cut and run for it. I suppose they'll borrow the Bristol, but it would be cheap at the price."

He stopped; but didn't win the smile he expected. Felicity was standing very still. He could see how pale and shocked she looked. There were dark patches beneath her eyes, but those eyes themselves were too bright; feverishly so. He looked at the empty cardigan sleeve, and for the first time since he had come into the room, something of his earlier grimness showed in his expression.

Yet it was Hanna who spoke next.

"They will never run away and leave you two alive," she announced, "they would rather kill themselves and kill you, too."

She spoke so simply.

Had she seemed excited, had she raised her voice, had she even raised a hand and tried to impress Dawlish, he might have laughed that off; but she did none of these things. Her great eyes were earnest to a point of solemnity. Her beauty was a marvel in itself, but nothing impressed him so much as the flat insistence of her voice, and the things that she said. She felt quite sure that rather than allow him and Felicity to escape alive, they would kill them and also kill themselves.

Dawlish felt the hand of fear resting coldly upon him.

He fought it back.

"There would be a little matter of how," he said; "I don't die really easily. Who are you?"

Hanna said, with the same flat, toneless voice: "I am—I *was* one of them. I came to try to help Mrs. Dawlish, because I knew that they meant to kill her, but—I don't think they'll take any notice of me, now."

Dawlish forced himself to speak quickly, lightly, as if he felt quite sure that there was nothing in the world to worry about, now.

"I think you're taking it too hard, you know, and they're not as good as you think they are."

"Oh, they can kill us all," Hanna said.

She didn't raise her voice or try to emphasize what she said, but was quite certain of herself. They could and they would kill everyone in this house, rather than allow anyone who had seen them to escape alive.

Felicity moved towards Dawlish.

He didn't speak again, but was feeling the effects of the strain, the shock and the gargantuan efforts he had made. He stood quite still, in a room which was as shadowy as it would be at dusk on an ordinary day. The wind smacked against the windows but the rain seemed to have slackened. There was Robert Marsh, at Alum Village by now with any luck, and the whole wide world outside—and just this little group of people here.

The girl believed that they would and could kill them all. How right was she?

CHAPTER XV

## THE FRIENDS OF DAWLISH

DAWLISH was an incalculable man. So were most of his friends. Those two men who had received the message which he had left for them in London were in their ways very different and yet they had much in common.

Among the things in common was a regard for and a devotion to Dawlish which was quite remarkable.

True, all three had served through three campaigns together, they had come close to dying together and, before and after the war, they had ventured together off the paths of peace and quiet. They had a gift, or a kink, call it what you will, of being able to forget that death might come to them. There were times when this was a great help to them; other times, when it made terror for their wives and developed into an evening's wrangling about the proper speed of cars on English roads, perhaps; or the degree of folly of following

Dawlish when he raised a little finger, and beckoned. It wasn't simply that they followed Dawlish, although they believed that he was a man to follow. The things he stood for and the things he did had a kind of siren call for them. Both men knew this. They also knew that they should, at times, resist it. Occasionally they even tried, but seldom very hard.

The first to receive the message was Tim Jeremy.

Tim, who had a small flat in a Mayfair mews—one in fact which had once been the communal property of Dawlish and these two and several others—was a very tall, lean man with a remarkable face. At times he was positively ugly, and at others he was almost handsome. No one could explain this metamorphosis, not even his wife. As luck would have it, his wife was out shopping, not at one of the big stores or in the small exclusive streets nearby, but at Shepherd Market, where goods—including vegetables—were reasonably cheap, and the fish and fowls as fresh as anywhere in London.

When the telephone rang Tim, sitting at a desk in a corner of a tiny room, and wrestling with certain unpalatable facts and figures to do with taxation, dropped a pencil with ready relief and picked the telephone up quickly; he appeared to be anxious that the caller should not ring off.

"Tim Jeremy here."

"Good morning, Mr. Jeremy," said the Carilon Club operator, "I am speaking for Major Dawlish."

The 'Major' told Tim that this was the Carilon Club, for, wherever possible, its staff clung to military ranks and titles of its members, forgetting that many were temporary.

The 'Dawlish', of course, made Tim's brown eyes kindle.

"That's good," he said.

The operator found herself stifling a laugh; of all the friends of Dawlish and members of the Carilon, Jeremy was most likely to bring a spontaneous grin.

"He asked me to ring you immediately," the girl said, "and he's *very* anxious that you should go to Alum, if it's at all possible."

Tim wrinkled his nose, like a bloodhound on the scent.

"At once?" he asked, as if mildly.

"Yes, sir. He said that it was very urgent, and that you will find a message at The Bull. I believe that is the name of an inn in Alum Village."

"A pub by any other name sells just the same," said Tim Jeremy, earnestly. "He didn't give you any indication of causes, did he? Trials, troubles, things like that?"

"He just said that it was very urgent—and he asked me to call Captain Beresford, too."

"Oh," said Tim, and now his thin nose with the rather full nostrils was wrinkling into deep furrows. "Sounds like a piece of cake," he mumbled, almost to himself. "Have you called Captain Beresford yet?"

"I will as soon as I've finished this call, sir."

"Bless your heart. Tell Captain Beresford that for private reasons—he'll know what I mean—I have to leave at once, and that if I don't see him on the road, I'll wait five minutes at the A.A. office at Guildford. Five, precisely, understood?"

"Fully, sir, yes."

"Fine," said Tim, and smiled and said, "Over to you."

He replaced the receiver and stood up with one and the same movement. Then, he picked up a pencil and a fresh sheet of paper, and scrawled on it: *Sorry, sweet, urgent call, piece of cake I shouldn't wonder. Expect me when I arrive.* He placed this prominently on the table where his wife could not possibly miss it, and then went into his bedroom. There, he crossed at once to the wardrobe, knelt down, and opened the drawer at the bottom; inside this drawer was a locked box. He unlocked it with a key from the dozen on his ring, and looked upon a small Webley automatic, a grey, deadly, snug-looking weapon. Packed with it were two clips of ammunition. He put one of these into the gun, slipped the other into his pocket, put the gun into another pocket so that it weighed his coat down a little, closed the drawer, and went out.

Now, his movements were not only hasty, but almost furtive.

He collected a trilby hat, two small blocks of chocolate from a drawer in the dining-room, and a whisky-flask which was already full. Thus accoutred, he went into the tiny hall and opened the door. At first, he opened it only an inch or so, giving himself just room to look out. The mews appeared to be empty. It was at once his fortune and his curse that the three garages in the mews were already let on long-term basis, so his car was garaged five minutes' walk away.

Today, he blessed it.

He nipped out of the mews, waving to a mechanic who was looking with remote interest at the engine of a Rolls-Bentley, and stepped into the narrow street which served the mews. Tall houses were on either side; iron grills at windows told of gloomy semi-basements, kitchens and cloakrooms. At the end of the road was another, where tall, graceful houses hid a view of one of London's parks.

Tim Jeremy turned right, and was at last fairly sure that he would not meet his wife. He had, of course, a feeling of guilt about this furtiveness, but it was a simple fact that if they met she would want to know where he was going, and when she knew, she would do everything reasonably possible to stop him. She was not the only woman in London for whom D stood for Danger and Dawlish almost simultaneously; and Tim preferred to apologize afterwards rather than explain beforehand.

He began to whistle, softly.

He reached another mews and his own car, an old, bright yellow Bentley. Not one of the sleek, opulent millionaire's cars of the new effete generation but an early vintage model with a front like a small steam engine, huge wheels, little body, and a super-charged engine. Even when he started the engine it was like listening to a jet. As he sat at the wheel, he smiled; and when he drove out he ignored all those people who stared at him, all the children who pointed, all the errand-boys who looked excited and all the policemen who looked knowing and hopeful. In fact, until he was out of the built-up area, at the top of Putney Hill, he drove with great circum-spection.

Then, he put his foot down.

He had at least a five minutes' start on Ted Beresford, and by the time he reached Guildford, that should be ten minutes.

And twenty at Alum! He might even know all about the show first.

With no thought of deadliness, but light-hearted and gay, he drove and whistled and, occasionally, munched a piece of chocolate; for he was sure there there would be no time to stop anywhere for lunch.

.        .        .        .        .

Ted Beresford was not at all like Tim Jeremy to look at. Tim was at times quite handsome, as we already know; Ted was perennially ugly. It was a genial kind of ugliness, and when women met him for the first time, they felt that they wanted to put their arms round him and pat his shoulder, as they would pat a Great Dane or a St. Bernard. He had that kind of look. His smile wrinkled his face, showed his fine, white teeth, told them of the easy generosity of his nature.

A slow man; sometimes.

He was, in fact, a little slower these days than he had been in the past, and that had not much to do with the passing of the years. He had lost a leg, while active on an affair with Dawlish. It had happened many years ago, and he had almost forgotten what it was like to have two whole legs; in fact his artificial one was so effective that he could perform tricks with it. One of the first things he had mastered was the driving of a car but, at his wife's pleading, he had not gone in for anything really fast; just a vintage Jaguar.

He received the message when he was in his small office in Albemarle Street. He ran a small exclusive travel agency, started when he had fallen on difficult days financially, and he had a staff of two; man and girl. They could cope. He gave them brief instructions, including one strict one: at five o'clock that afternoon, and not a minute before, they were to telephone his wife and tell her that he might be back late, for he had gone to Alum Village to see the Dawlishes.

"And remember, the plural," he insisted. "It always sounds more respectable that way."

"Yes, Mr. Beresford!"

"Happy days," said Beresford, gloomily, and walked out. No one meeting him casually would have guessed that he had an artificial leg. He nipped down the stairs like a two-year-old, and whistled when he reached the sunlit street. The wind was coming from the west and the bad weather hadn't yet struck this heart of London.

"Eeenie-meenie miney-mo," crooned Beresford, "catch a bad man by his toe. Wonder what it is." He smiled, as if at the most happy prospect he could imagine. "Wonder if I'll need a rocket?" He shrugged. "I can borrow one from Pat if it's that kind of show."

By rocket, he meant a gun.

His car was parked in Berkeley Square, where he was on excellent terms with the attendants, who welcomed him warmly.

"Coming back, sir?" one of them asked.

"Shouldn't think so, today," said Beresford. "Not until late afternoon, anyhow." He had a little difficulty in getting into the car, not because of his leg but because of his bulk. He was a large man. That, of course, was also true of Dawlish, but in a different way. Dawlish was lean—well, leanish. Beresford was very nearly fat, and had a big, clumsy-looking figure. But once at the wheel he was snug and comfortable.

He knew that Tim Jeremy knew all about this.

He had heard, wryly, the message about meeting at the A.A. Office at Guildford, which was on the approach to the by-pass. The 'five minutes' told him that Tim would be off like a bullet on the sixtieth second of the fifth minute, and hoped—in fact intended—to get to Alum first. That might be wise, even if it was not particularly friendly.

Beresford, like Jeremy, knew nothing at all of the situation at Alum and Four Ways. He felt almost as light-hearted as Jeremy, and would have been quite as light-hearted had he been able to start out first. Still, there it was. Unless something fell off the old Bentley Tim would get to Alum a quarter of an hour ahead of him.

Queer.

Why pick up a message at The Bull? Why not at Four Ways itself?

Beresford, threading his way through the traffic near Sloane Square, was asking himself this very thoughtfully. He had known Dawlish for nearly twenty years, and although it was some time since he had received this kind of message from him, memory of past occasions was vivid; in fact, a part of existence.

Pat didn't want him to go straight to the house.

So . . .

Pat didn't want Felicity to know that anything was brewing.

Beresford reached that happy conclusion, smiled seraphically and settled down to the drive. Traffic was much thinner now, and he was making surprising speed. With a little luck, he would pick up five minutes getting out of Town, and if he managed to do that then he might get to Guildford before the five minutes' grace was up.

In fact, he would.

From Esher, he really put his foot down. There wasn't a lot of traffic, and most of it was slow. The Jaguar had one of those moods which made it easy for fans to say that the earliest models were the best. It purred and flew along, and there were moments when Beresford believed that he not only had a chance to get to the rendezvous before Tim arrived, but might actually pass him on the road. Now that would really be an achievement. He put his foot down harder, and ripped along.

Soon, he was within sight of the signposts at the approach to the by-pass. He hadn't passed Tim, which was sad, but if Tim had gone on he'd be mad. It wouldn't be playing the game. Nothing on four wheels . . .

He reached the roundabout.

Tim hadn't gone on, but was on the far side, standing by the antediluvian yellow monster, waving his arms as if in protest and with argument. By his side, half a head shorter, were two patrol policemen in their neat blue uniforms, and just in front of the Bentley was a police-car.

Ted stared—and grinned.

He had never looked or felt happier.

He slowed down, until the black Jaguar was crawling at a pace which would have shamed a motor-scooter. He did not want to make the slightest unnecessary sound or draw attention even for a moment. He would not attempt to attract Tim's attention. It was a pity, but all this was in the luck of the game, and if Tim had come across the same situation, he would probably have waved as he had driven by.

That would be insult to injury.

Must be quite a show. Two motor-cycle cops were a little way ahead of the Bentley, their riders sitting on them, ready to pounce. Speed trap, of course. Oh, well, accidents were accidents and someone had to do something about them. He would creep through Guildford, but once on the open road beyond—*swiiiish!*

He passed the cops.

Then, to his horror, one of them shouted. He pretended not to notice and put his foot down hard; not to have done so would have been more than flesh and blood could stand. But the staccato snort of the police motor-cycle soon sounded clearly. The mirror told him that both were after him, and catching up. By then, he was slowing down, and becoming indignant. He had crept round at twenty-five, it wasn't until they had started to chase him that he had put on speed. That was a form of *agent provocateur*-ing, and he would say his piece with vigour.

He pulled in.

One motor-cyclist stopped alongside.

"Sorry to pull you up, sir," he said mildly, "but we've had a request from the Yard. Should be someone along to see you soon, sir. Message was for both you and Mr. Jeremy—you *are* Mr. Beresford, aren't you?"

Ted said, sharply: "Yes. Not trouble, is it?"

"I honestly can't say, sir," said the motor-cycle cop, "we were just told to keep you here, that's all."

## CHAPTER XVI

# TALK OF EXILES

DAWLISH stood with his Felicity in the bedroom, and both of them looked at Hanna. She seemed so very young. She obviously meant exactly what she said, too; at least, she appeared to believe it. There was a kind of intensity about her which couldn't be mistaken and couldn't be scoffed at. That aloofness remained, but it no longer mattered.

Downstairs, there was a silence.

Outside, after the lull, the rain was coming down faster and spattering against the windows and running down them in small torrents.

Dawlish gave Felicity's waist a little extra squeeze and said:

"Well, we may as well sit down while we try to sort it out." There were two armchairs, a chair without arms for sewing, and a dressing-table stool. Dawlish chose the stool. He saw Felicity sit down heavily, and guessed just how near she was to despair. He wondered what was really going on in the other girl's mind. "When you say you're one of 'them'," he went on quietly, "what do you mean exactly?"

She hesitated.

Dawlish thought that he heard a movement outside, but couldn't be sure. He didn't move. He needed a few minutes' rest, and there would be plenty of warning before anyone tried to get into the room; even with a battering ram, it would take five minutes.

The girl was standing by the side of the chair; she didn't sit down.

"My name is Hanna of Goetz," she said clearly. "You will perhaps have heard of Goetz."

Dawlish said, "Vaguely," and stopped.

"That is how most people have heard of it," said Hanna of Goetz, and she smiled a little, almost wearily. "It is, of course, a very small country, little more than a principality, and it has been almost forgotten since we were—absorbed."

Dawlish thought, 'It's coming back.'

There were San Marino, Liechtenstein, Luxemburg—and Goetz. It had been a principality with its own ruling prince, a tiny relic from the Europe of the days before the independent states had merged with the large ones; and it had been one of the few which had kept its independence until the beginning of the Second World War. Then, it had vanished under the torrent. When the Yugo-Slav defection from the Comintern had startled the world, there had been rumours that Goetz would also free itself, not being important enough to be forced to stay within the framework of the dominant states. Nothing had transpired.

The simple truth was that Goetz was too small to win much sympathy anywhere; it had been absorbed, it was a memory; but there, as well as everywhere, the Freedom Movement had existed and it was known that the Prince of Goetz had been living in exile for many years.

It was almost a common or garden story.

Certainly there was nothing particularly remarkable about it, and because the Princes of Goetz had ruled with reasonable efficiency and humanity, the principality had seldom been in the public eye. No romantic monarch had ridden across the world's Press from Goetz—and the royal family was so little known that except in places where the old rules were followed, its members were hardly acknowledged.

And this was Hanna of Goetz.

She went on: "A few months ago, my uncle—the prince—died, Mr. Dawlish. He was in exile, of course, like all of us. His son, Josef, then became the prince. Josef now is—downstairs perhaps near death himself."

Felicity said, "*Prince* Josef," in a hollow voice.

"Yes," said Hanna, in much more matter-of-fact tone. "He is my cousin, and so young. . . ." She moved suddenly, and went to the window, as if she was no longer even slightly afraid of what might happen if anyone saw her. She stood looking out, and did not appear to notice Dawlish get up from the stool and move towards her. "I wished that he had given up his throne, given up pretending, but they wouldn't let him."

Dawlish was just behind her.

He put his hands on her shoulders, to draw her to one side, out of range should anyone there decide to have a go. She glanced round at him with sudden anger. "Why do you touch me?"

"That's a bad place to stand," Dawlish said.

Her anger faded, but she did not move.

"I am not afraid," she said proudly.

Dawlish didn't touch her again, but waited. With a shrug, she moved away from the window, and Dawlish went back to his seat.

Hanna went on:

"But they wouldn't let him. Otto and Emil were his counsellors. They had served his father for years, in exile, and Josef had no one else to turn to for advice. Is it surprising that he did what they suggested?" She turned round and flung the question out, so sharply and tensely that it startled Felicity.

Dawlish said, "It sounds reasonable to me." He wanted to know what had happened to this Prince Josef, what he was doing downstairs, how he was, how seriously she meant that the youth was near death; but if he interrupted too often it might stop her from talking, and once she stopped, she might not begin again. He knew that she was able to explain the *why* of all this; and once he knew that he might have a chance to fight back.

He wondered how many men were here.

He wondered, still, how right she was when she said that they—this man Otto and this Emil—could and would kill them all.

What were they doing now? What were they planning? Why was the house so silent, after the tumult of his arrival? Were they just licking their wounds or were they planning this new attack which Hanna of Goetz expected?

Her glittering grey eyes looked as if they were aching unbearably.

"Of course he was advised by them, at first," she said. "They had advised his father; he had no one else to turn to, and was very young. Do you know how old Josef is?" She flung that out as a kind of challenge.

"I've never seen and hardly heard of him," Dawlish said quietly.

"He is twenty-one," Hanna told him sharply, "and he has been kept apart from other people most of his life; instead of allowing him to mix with them, to make friends, to understand them, they kept him apart, alone. I was allowed to come to England and to be educated here, but not Josef. He was kept in a lonely exile in North Africa, he had private tutors, he learned everything—*everything*—except how to live and how to become a human being. He was taught to look on himself as a prince ordained to rule, he was kept in ignorance of the real issues in the world, he——"

Hanna broke off.

Dawlish made himself sit there, fighting back his impatience with curiosity. If he faced the truth, there was little that he could do but wait. Just wait. . . .

There were Ted and Tim. There was Bob Marsh. There was the hour's grace that he had asked for, but allowing the girl to talk as the words came into her head, allowing her to overcome that natural reluctance to talk, would not make very much difference.

Five minutes?

She seemed to sense his anxiety, for she turned round and faced him, spreading her hands out in front of her, and saying:

"I am taking too long to tell you. I will try to hurry." When she spoke like that she betrayed the fact that English wasn't her mother tongue. Her beauty was more Slav than English, after all, and it seemed touched with tragedy. In spite of her words, she was silent again for a full minute; then she went on very firmly: "It is simply this: over the years, Otto and Emil have been plotting for a return to the throne. Oh, I knew it, everyone suspected it, but is that so unusual? Most deposed monarchs plan to go back; all of them have their advisers, to whom plotting and spying and intriguing are like food and drink. For little Goetz, it was laughable! Comical! The prince —he is really our King—believed in it and Josef was made to believe in it—he was brought up to feel certain that he was destined to return to Goetz as the ruling prince, and that he was heir to all its wealth.

"Its wealth," Hanna repeated softly; "and it is very rich. For centuries, gold and jewels had been hoarded against such a day as came. In recent years, most of the gold was used to buy jewels, for easy transportation. The prince was wise so far, but—what he did not know, what none of us realized, was that Otto and Emil had brought much of this wealth away. It was easy to smuggle across some frontiers, at others bribes were used, in others it was a matter of good fortune. This great wealth was brought out a little at a time, and with it Otto and Emil had been paying agents to go to Goetz and form a resistance movement.

"Then, two things happened. First, the new rulers of Goetz discovered the plot. There was a purge—you must remember it," Hanna said urgently, and in fact Dawlish did: and now he knew where he had heard of Prince Josef and Goetz before. A day's sensation in the newspapers, so quickly forgotten.

He nodded.

"The men who had been working with Otto and Emil were executed," Hanna went on, "and it became obvious that Josef would never be able to go there as ruler—or, in fact, as anything. No one in Goetz wanted the ruling prince. Now that Otto and Emil had been drawing on the wealth of the country, the peasants and the factory workers felt that they had been cheated; even if there had been a chance before, there was none now.

"Josef was never a fool.

"He heard about this from one of the men who had escaped from Goetz. He did not talk to Otto or Emil, at first, but studied the situation closely. He realized that these men still had control of a fortune, which was rightly his—or his people's. I do not think," Hanna went on very quietly, "that it would ever be possible to make Josef believe that they were *not* his people, whether they acknowledged him or not."

Dawlish said quietly, "I can understand that."

Felicity didn't speak, but watched the girl intently as if every word she uttered was important. It was possible to believe that she had forgotten their situation: the men down-stairs; the men outside; the talk and the very threat of death.

It would be easy to forget; the girl held them as a great actress could hold ten thousand, driving out all realities except the reality of her presence.

All was quiet below; suspiciously quiet.

"It was not long before he made another discovery, and in this I was able to help him," Hanna went on, quietly. "Otto believed in the future of the ruling house, he lived for it and for nothing else. If that were to fail, then everything would fail. I wonder," Hanna went on very slowly, "if you can imagine such a thing happening to a man? He is loyal and faithful, he loves the people whom he serves, he sees their misfortunes, he struggles with them, he shares their dangers, he shares their exile, he schemes and plots and dreams of nothing but the day when they will return to what he believes to be theirs by right—even by *divine* right."

Her voice challenged Dawlish.

He said, "Yes, I can imagine it."

"There, then, is Otto," said Hanna, proudly. "After the death of the old prince, there was Josef. Josef became not a young man of flesh and blood, not a human being, but a kind of symbol, almost a kind of god. Once he was back on the throne, Otto would bring himself to believe that his life's work was done; but until then the plotting must go on. The purge mattered nothing. Otto did not care who was killed, did not care what sacrifices anyone made. He was prepared to sacrifice everything so why shouldn't others do the same?

"He plotted another revolt.

"He still had agents, and wanted to stir them to a wild attempt to take over the country. It would take years and it would take a fortune and he, Otto, had control of that fortune. All that was needed, then, was the time and the patience and the figurehead, the symbol of liberty and freedom—Josef.

"Josef had to become not only a dream but a saint. The

whole plot had to be built round him, he had to become the idol of everyone in Goetz, rich and poor, peasant and town-worker. That was what he had been groomed for—a prince more regal than any of the century.

"But Otto forgot one thing.

"Otto forgot that Josef had a mind.

"Josef studied everything, discovered what had happened, decided that it would be folly to attempt to go back, and—he found where it was and took away the great fortune which had been amassed by Otto and the others. No one knows where he sent it. It was known that he had some receipt, some papers, which might enable the jewels to be traced. And Otto discovered what he had done after Josef fled to this country. Otto, Emil and several other men followed him, but Josef made it clear that he would not return to Goetz, that they were wasting their time in trying to make him. When Otto realized that, he knew there was only one thing to do. Find Josef, and the hiding place of the wealth, and find out who else Josef had told about these things.

"It was impossible for Josef to work through ordinary channels," Hanna went on, quietly. "He was just a princeling exile, and no one had much time for him. In fact, the Western governments were nervous of any association with him. Goetz could become a kind of—kind of——" She broke off, searching for a word.

"Flash-point," Dawlish offered.

Hanna's eyes lit up.

"Yes, that is the word—a flash-point! Josef was not, of course, recognized. He did not have permission to come into this country, but among his friends was one who helped him here and who told him to come to you. Another, when questioned, told Otto and Emil of this."

Hanna raised her voice as she said that.

Except for the rain, there was no other sound.

It would be easy to ask her who had sent Josef to Dawlish, but that didn't matter. If he was to be sent to anyone in this country who might help, then Dawlish was as likely as any. Dawlish's reputation spread world-wide, on either side of every curtain, everywhere. No, it did not greatly matter who had sent Prince Josef to this house.

Not now.

Then Hanna went on:

"That is really everything," she said, "except that he was found in England and soon followed. Today, there was an accident, when Emil and Otto caught up with him. He was shot, but he escaped and came here——"

"Who shot him?" Dawlish asked quietly.

She said, "I do not know, I was not present, but I understood he was to be frightened, and the 'accident' happened."

Did she believe that?

Whatever she knew to be true, she wasn't likely to alter her story yet.

"Otto and Emil hurried after him—well, you know what happened next," Hanna went on. "Otto believes he brought the documents, the secret of the lost wealth, and Otto will do everything he can to get them. He thinks it possible you were entrusted with these documents, but his real belief is that Josef brought them here, and that your wife hid them." Hanna glanced at Felicity, but did not even ask if that were true. "What you have to understand is that if Otto cannot get what he wants, he will *kill*. If he has no chance of doing what he wants to do, he will make sure that we all die. He has only the one thing to live for, and if he cannot get it, then he will kill himself and take everyone he can with him. Oh, he *can* do that." Doubt must have shown in Dawlish's eyes, for Hanna quickened her words as she went on: "He is always prepared. For himself, and for Emil and the other men, poison. What is it—cyanide, yes, cyanide. For us, and this house—perhaps he will set fire to it, perhaps he will blow it up. It is possible these days to carry very powerful explosives in the pocket, isn't it?"

It was.

"And of course," Hanna went on, "if Otto should get the documents, he will be wild with delight, and so grateful, *your* danger will be much less. You would not have to die."

She finished, watching first Dawlish and then Felicity.

Dawlish stood up slowly, and the movement stopped
Hanna. He didn't go towards her, but said very quietly:

"Hanna, I can believe all this because of what's happened,
I can even believe that Otto will try to kill us, but—how do
you know about it all? Why should Otto confide in you?"

She raised her hands; her imperiousness and her arrogance
had never shown more plainly.

"Surely that is obvious," she said. "I am Josef's cousin.
After Josef, I would inherit the throne."


CHAPTER XVII

ULTIMATUM

THERE was nothing to say to Hanna.

It seemed so obvious that she told the truth, at least about
her identity. And it would explain how she knew everything,
why she was so vital to Otto and his men.

She put her hands to her cheeks and thrust her hair back,
a gesture which threw her beauty into greater relief, which
made her look more goddess than princess. Every movement
she made had a quality which it was easy to understand now;
and to explain.

"Now I have told you," she said. "I came up here, Mr.
Dawlish, because I would not allow them to kill—to kill your
wife, if it could be avoided. I came to tell her that it might be
possible to buy her safety, if only she would tell Otto where
the papers are."

Dawlish looked gently at Felicity, and there was a glow
in his eyes.

"My sweet, have you held out all this time?"

"Pat," said Felicity, helplessly, "I wish I had, I wish I
knew where the papers are, but I don't. Prince—Prince Josef
didn't give them to me. I've never had them. All I know . . ."
She told him, in almost unbelieving tones, a little of what had
happened, how she had first seen Josef stumbling towards

her, and how she had gone to help. Her word pictures were vivid, her story almost unbelievable and yet demonstrably true.

"*Is* it true?" Hanna asked, and caught her breath. "You really do not know where those documents are?"

"I just don't know," Felicity insisted.

"But Josef had them, we know he had them!" Hanna cried out. "That is quite certain. He had them and he came here and—they were in his pocket. He gave us one packet, a false one—you *must* have had them, you must have hidden them!"

Her eyes were almost condemning.

Felicity said, "I know nothing at all about them."

Hanna moved back. "I—I cannot understand," she said, and made the gesture with her hair again. "It is crazy, it is unbelievable. Surely he did have them? Or . . ." She looked at Dawlish accusingly.

"All of this is absolute news to me," he said.

She took her hands from her face and held them out beseechingly. "If you know, you must tell us where they are. Don't you understand what I say? Those papers will give you a chance, perhaps your only chance, to escape from here."

"I don't *know* where they are!" Felicity cried.

Dawlish watched the two women, and marvelled—much less at Hanna than at Felicity. After all this, after the hours of mental anguish, of physical fear and sharp danger, she could stand there and say almost apologetically: "I don't *know* where they are." She must have realized the significance of the documents, and all that they might mean, but she hardly seemed to consider that: she didn't fly off into near hysteria, or beat her breast, or, stung by the challenge, raise her voice or lose her temper. She just said flatly that she didn't know.

"*Is* that possible?" Hanna asked, and she seemed to be talking to herself. "All this, for—but where did he put them, where are they?"

Dawlish said dryly, "Apparently only Josef knows."

Hannah didn't speak, but moved towards the window again.

Dawlish went ahead and drew the curtains, without a word; the night was shut out. Then he switched on a bedside lamp, and Felicity switched on the light by the door.

"Why do you shut out the daylight?" Hanna asked.

"So that they can't see you, or see us," Dawlish said dryly.

Now, for the first time, there was a sound near the door—and it seemed to Dawlish that a dozen things happened at once, all demanding quick attention. Men were moving about more freely, downstairs. He raised a curtain, to look out cautiously, as he heard men coming up the stairs. One moved into sight in the garden—one of the guards, who turned and faced the house and this room. They were making it more obvious that they were surrounding the room. Another man started the engine of the Californian, and it appeared, moving slowly down the drive. Near the gates, it was stopped. Obviously, that was put there to make sure that no car could swing into the drive and repeat Dawlish's performance.

Dawlish was watching Hanna—the heir presumptive to a non-existent kingdom. She seemed as if she was struggling to accept the truth of what Felicity had told her, but wasn't really sure.

He said, almost brusquely, "How ill is Josef?"

"Very ill," Hanna said, "the doctor did not think he would live." She moved forward, slowly, looking lost and helpless. "I do not know what to do now. I had hoped that if your wife would tell Otto where to find the documents, it would be possible to make him go away without—without killing her. I was prepared——"

She broke off.

A man was at the landing, now; and a second arrived. The movements were quite audible, and there was no doubt that they were there. What were they planning? Dawlish watched the door behind the two beds, and spoke softly to Hanna.

"What were you prepared to do?"

She said simply: "I was going to tell him that I would not allow murder, that I would stay behind with your wife until he and Emil and the others were gone. At least that would have given you some chance. Now . . ."

The footsteps came closer, and there was a sharp tap at the door.

Felicity jumped.

Dawlish began to smile.

"Parley plea," he prophesied. "They want those papers badly, don't they?" 'Parley' was almost certainly right, and it meant more time, at least. He didn't say another word to either of the women but went a little closer to the door, and called. "Anyone there?"

"Mr. Dawlish," a man said in a dry voice, "I wish to talk to you."

"*Otto*," breathed Hanna.

"Otto," said Dawlish, "I'm listening."

"Mr. Dawlish," said Otto, in the same dry, precise voice, "I wish you to understand that it will not help you to stay behind locked door. It is much better to come out and discuss the situation."

"Good idea," said Dawlish, "just as soon as the police arrive, I'll come out and talk. Then, there'll be the policemen in control. Tomorrow, the magistrates. The——"

"Mr. Dawlish," Otto began again, in exactly the same tone, "It will not assist you to be facetious. You are helpless in there. The room is surrounded. If you should appear at the window, you will be shot. If you try to come out of the door, it will be likewise. But if you are sensible and come and discuss this matter with us——"

"I'll only get my throat cut," Dawlish said.

There was silence.

Hanna pressed her hands to the sides of her head, and looked despairingly from Dawlish to Felicity, went towards her, began to speak in a whisper, and then broke off. Felicity didn't know what she had been going to say.

"Mr. Dawlish," Otto called, "it is very simple. We need the papers which the wounded man gave to Mrs. Dawlish. Nothing else. We will take nothing of yours. Give us those papers and we shall go."

"No papers," said Dawlish.

In a whisper, Hanna breathed, "But if Mrs. Dawlish hasn't got them——"

Dawlish put a hand out, and held her arm, firmly. She stopped speaking. There was another pause, before Otto went on very clearly and firmly:

"Why are you not sensible, Dawlish? If you give us the papers we shall leave here, and you and your wife will not be hurt. If you refuse . . ." It was possible to see the lines at his face and forehead get deeper, and to imagine the way he shrugged his shoulders. "Be sensible, Dawlish, there is no other way of helping yourself."

"What I have, I hold," Dawlish announced.

Hanna breathed, "Tell him you haven't got them, then it may be——" She broke off.

"Mr. Dawlish," Otto said, "we shall allow you ten minutes to consider this further. I want you to understand exactly what I mean. We shall not leave here without these documents. We shall leave no one at this house alive, and little of the house shall be left standing. Imagine what that means, Mr. Dawlish. Your wife dead, your home destroyed, all the things you love in flames, until there is nothing but charred ashes, only the remains of all the things which are dear to you. Why are you so stubborn? These papers mean nothing to you, but they mean much to us. Let us have them, and we will go in peace."

Dawlish waited for a few seconds, and then said in a different tone of voice:

"Otto, would you like to know something?"

"Please, yes!"

"Would you like to know my terms?"

"*Please!*" There was sharp excitement in the man's voice.

"Go and fetch Dr. Scott and bring him back to life," said Dawlish, in a steely voice. "When you've done that, I'll come and talk to you."

There was a sharp exclamation on the other side of the door; next a whisper of voices; then, silence. Boards creaked, and Dawlish knew that the two men were going away.

He ran his hand across his forehead.

From the side of the window he looked outside, and saw the guard watching, in that teeming rain.

Hanna came to him, swiftly: "I don't understand, you have let him think that you have those papers. Now you have no chance at all."

"Unless he thinks it better not to burn us and the papers," murmured Dawlish.

She closed her eyes.

"Yes—yes, it was foolish of me. Mr. Dawlish, please understand. I hate the thought of violence and bloodshed; if I had known what was going to happen I would never have come. I would rather die myself than have your wife killed here, or you, or—anyone else, in the name of Goetz." Her eyes were rounded and seemed to burn with the intensity of her feelings as she took his hands tightly, and then went on: "Let *me* go and talk to Otto. I can tell him that you were bluffing, I can make sure that he knows you haven't the papers. Then I believe that I can persuade him to leave without more bloodshed. If once he has reason to relieve that I will desert him——"

"Oh, no," said Dawlish, and smiled at her broadly, as if there were no need for alarm. "You stay right here. You're precious. You're *very* precious. I grant you that you may be the one to save our lives, but not your way. Bird in the hand," he almost burbled, and Hanna stared at him as if she thought he had lost his wits. "Do I gather that Otto doesn't know you're here?"

"No, he does not. I told him that I must rest, that my head was aching. I came in stealthily." She looked across at Felicity, as if for confirmation.

Felicity nodded.

Dawlish said softly: "Bless your heart, you don't know how much good you've done me! You'll stay here, though, and next time Otto comes to bargain perhaps he'll get a shock. Perhaps." He grinned, and again looked almost foolish. "Any idea what he will do when the police arrive?"

Felicity broke in, "Did you tell them, Pat?"

"Oh, they'll soon know all about it," Dawlish assured her. "I left a message for Tim and Ted at The Bull, too, so we'll have both kinds of help soon. It isn't all so easy for Otto as it looks," he added, for Hanna's benefit. "What is your guess, Princess Hanna? What do you think he will do when the police arrive?"

Hanna said flatly: "I think he will destroy this house and everything and everyone in it. If there is any way in which you can keep your friends away, then you should do it."

Felicity, by Dawlish's side, gripped his arm.

He was still smiling, but it was a set smile.

He said, "You could be right, but will he want you to go too?"

"If you were dealing with a man of sanity, it might be possible to expect him to be logical," Hanna said, "but I tell you that unless he can do what he wants, unless he can carry out his mission, then he will kill himself and everyone and everything else he can. I am *quite* sure." She didn't move or touch Dawlish this time, but went on very flatly: "Why do you not believe me? I might be able to persuade him that if we leave here, now, we shall be able to win another chance. No one else can possibly persuade him. I do not think there is any way to stop him."

She stopped.

Dawlish looked at Felicity, and knew that Felicity was already half-convinced that their only chance rested in this girl.

Did it?

## CHAPTER XVIII

## GREAT MAN

BACK at Guildford, Ted Beresford got out of his Jaguar when he realized that the motor-cyclists meant exactly what they said, and would not allow him to go on. Tim Jeremy was already out of the Bentley. For the first time since he had been stopped he looked not only human but amused. He was in one of his good-looking phases, with a healthy colour and a glint in his brown eyes. As Ted was massively built, so Tim was painfully thin.

They strolled towards each other.

Less than an hour's drive away, at the house which they knew very well, Dawlish had just smashed his way into the hall. Less than an hour's drive away, Bob Marsh had reached The Bull, and was sitting in the kitchen behind the public rooms, with a whisky in front of him, and a wide-eyed innkeeper and his wife watching the horror in his eyes and the fear on his face. He hadn't yet tried to explain what had happened, and was still breathing hard. The Vauxhall was outside The Bull, and the prisoner was still in the boot; Dawlish hadn't told the innkeeper about him.

And at the roundabout which led to the Guildford by-pass, Tim grinned broadly as Ted approached him, and Ted began to smile with the same kind of delight.

Tim broke the silence.

"That old crock of yours broken down?" he asked. "I waited for a couple of centuries, if I hadn't I'd have been on the way before the cops got here."

That, patently, was a lie.

Ted kept a blandly straight face. "No, it wasn't trouble with the car that delayed me," he answered, "it was the vibration. You know the kind of thing."

Tim stopped smiling, suspecting a trap, and seeking it.

"Did you say vibration?"

"That's the word. Vibration."

"What kind of vibration?" Tim asked, cautiously.

"Road vibration," Ted said sweetly. "There's far too much heavy old stuff on the road, I could feel the shivers your steam engine was giving me miles behind. Not fallen to pieces yet?"

They grinned.

They shook hands.

"Any idea what this is all about?" asked Ted, as they strolled together towards the Bentley. "Pat must be in pretty deep or they wouldn't have the cops out."

"All I know is a call from the club."

"Same here," said Ted. "Didn't know Pat was up to anything, did you?"

"No."

"The man's a menace," announced Ted. "Not telling us, I mean. Anyhow, when he got into a jam he tried us, that's in his favour. Hallo, rain." He looked up at the clouds which were massing up—twenty miles away, at Four Ways, they were opening and rain was drenching the grounds and pouring down the windows. Ted's voice was pitched on a very low key, and none of the four policemen heard anything of what he said —all four were watching from a distance, and all four seemed amused, for they had heard of Dawlish and his friends. "Going to pelt down in a minute," Ted went on. "Tim."

"Hm?"

"How'd you feel? Venturesome?"

"Don't get it," said Tim Jeremy. "Explain."

"Well, why let them get away with this?" asked Ted reasoningly. "Work it out. If Pat had wanted the coppers on this show, he wouldn't have sent for us, would he? He saw it as something which we ought to handle *à trois*, so to speak. You know, the three of us. How's the old Bent for a quick start?"

Tim began to understand, and a smile dawned in his eyes, a seraphic glow which Ted saw and comprehended and fully approved.

"You mean," Tim said, "we could sit in."

"First, you could show me the works," agreed Ted. "Well, some of them. Point out its beauty. Brass and bright bits, too. Then we could get in and make ourselves comfortable."

"Light a cigarette, perhaps," suggested Tim.

"Or a pipe. Yes. Look leisurely. Tell you what," added Ted, as if inspired, "we could yawn. It's about time for the post-prandial." He yawned, realistically. "See what I mean? They'll just look at the two old men, and——"

"I drive off."

"S'right," said Ted. "That is, if she'll start."

"To date," said Tim, "I'll have you remember that we've

kept this party clean. The thing is, don't rush anything. Look earnest. Talking about something serious—you know, causes for alarm."

"Could curse a bit at the delay," said Ted. "It will look natural. Eh?"

"Good notion. And then for the sober topic—what about Pat? How about giving them a load of he's going to be the next Chief Copper? He is, isn't he? Scare 'em a bit, perhaps. You never know. Worth trying?"

"I'm with you," Ted said. "Nothing beats——"

He broke off.

Another car swung round the roundabout, and it was travelling at more than a reasonable speed. Any self-respecting traffic cop should bridle. It was chauffeur-driven and it had an English number-plate and the magic letters CD on it. Instead of hurtling past them, however, it turned towards them, and Ted Beresford whistled as it drew nearer, and said:

"Hallo. Corps Diplomatique. Who——"

Tim was staring at the man behind the chauffeur.

"Look," he breathed. "Fraud."

"Eh?"

"Fraud. Don't you see who that is? The Great Waffler. Pat's cousin, the chief copper-maker." Tim rubbed his chin very softly and very thoughtfully when he recognized the passenger and Ted, having also recognized him, gave a subdued whistle. They were, of course, as irreverent and disrespectful as any pair of club page-boys might be, even when the Home Secretary in person appeared; and yet they regarded him with a certain awe, accorded him a position and prestige. So, they realized that for him to arrive, in person, was quite remarkable. He had, it was known, invited Dawlish to become the Commissioner at Scotland Yard, but this was hardly concern for his future. It enlarged the scope of what was happening, and it fully explained the attitude of the police.

The chauffeur jumped out. The Great Waffler opened his window, and called:

"Spare me a minute, you two, will you? Plenty of room. Open the door, Symes."

"Yes, sir." The chauffeur sprang.

"Delighted," said Tim, "and I speak for both of us." His reaction was so subdued that it told its own story. They got in. It was a car which shall be nameless and there was room not for four in the back, but for six; and ample leg-room, too. The glass partition was up. The chauffeur got in, and the Great Waffler, a plump, pasty, sad-eyed man, tapped at it. "Just going off the main road," he explained. "If I stay here you can be sure that half Fleet Street will pass. A local Tory, anyhow." His voice added to his general impression of gloom, which was at least as much assumption as real. The car moved off, slowly. "I heard you'd been telephoned from the Club and asked to hurry down to Pat's place—rang the Club to find what I could. How much do you know of the idiot's part in *this* affair?"

No one asked whom he meant by 'idiot'.

"Nowt," said Ted.

"That the truth?"

"Sir," said Tim, very quietly, "there are times when we play the fool. This is not one of them. We had a message from Pat, this morning. Through the Club. He wanted us to pick up a message at The Bull, at Alum. That is, a pub. We were on our way when the police force decided that we had to be stopped."

"Yes," said the Great Waffler. "My fault, and it is not because I want to keep the idiot's nose clean." His eyes were half closed and his hands, the fingers interlaced, were spread over his middling paunch. "So you know nothing at all—not what it is or who it is?"

"Nothing."

"Hm," said the Great Waffler, expressively. "Pity. However, we might get something at The Bull. I say 'we' in its broad sense, I'm not coming any further, but I thought that if I had a word with you two I'd find out what you knew." He didn't move. The car had turned into a driveway, and come to a standstill; the chauffeur was as motionless as a statue of Mithras. The Great Waffler's eyes were half-closed, and nothing more was needed to tell Tim and Ted that he was really worried.

He opened his eyes wide.

"Can tell you this," he said. "An exiled monarch was smuggled into England. Caused a lot of diplomatic troubles. I could go into detail about why we've kept him out, but I won't. Thing is, he made a bee-line for Pat. Had a secret report from Intelligence an hour ago. This prince was advised to see Pat, it proved. Then, there was some kind of trouble at Alum. We had a man on the alert there, of course, and so did the other interested parties." A quirk of a smile appeared at his lips, but not for long. "The simple thing is that we would very much like to get the exiled prince and everyone with him out of the country quickly and without a lot of fuss. We don't mind any fuss the newspapers kick up afterwards. They're almost sure to, freedom and political asylum and all that, but you know." He unlaced two fingers and waggled them. "However, things went wrong. I've had a report from Alum. Our chap was shot at. There's real trouble at Pat's house. The lid's blown off—remember we're dealing with fanatics. We know that some of the people after the exile here are a bit bats. Barmy. Idealists. Or," went on the Great Waffler, relenting, "fanatics. Latest reports show that one of them has said that he'll put the exile back on the throne, or else. There's a lot of money and jewels involved, too, claimed by (a) the exile and (b) the proletariat. We can get our fingers burned down to the quick if we're not careful, and I want to know what's on there. Something badly wrong—had the place watched and reports have been telephoned, we don't always sleep in Whitehall, in spite of what that idiot——"

The Great Waffler broke off.

Then, he told them slowly:

"The simple truth is, I think that Pat's in a lot of trouble, whether he knew what he was doing or not. Felicity, too. But it's a delicate business, and if we *can* sort it out without kicking up too much of a shindy, we'd like to. So, I wanted a word with you two, first. We can send the police of even Special Branch and M.I.F. wallahs there, but we'd rather hold off unless we know that it's vital. As you two were sticking your heads out, anyhow——"

Again the Great Waffler broke off, and again the quirk of a smile touched his full lips.

The friends of Dawlish stared at him for what seemed a long, long time. Then, as in one breath, they said:

"Yes."

A pause.

"Thanks," added Tim.

"Can now understand that you and the idiot boy have common ancestry," said Ted. He could not have given higher praise. "One thing I don't quite get, though. Do I gather that you are not having the house itself watched?"

"Oh, yes, from a distance," said the Home Secretary. "Had a chap there when rumours about this prince wanting to see Pat came in a few days ago. Understand it properly, mind you, not the Home Office—Intelligence. The proper authority is." He smiled again. "I'm in this because I know Pat and because I thought I might short-cut things with you two. Take it from me, there is a lot of trouble at Four Ways. The indications are that Felicity's been there all the morning, held at pistol point, so to speak, and that Pat broke in just now. Literally. Had the report on the radio as I turned the corner to see you. Thing is, the pair of you with Pat might be able to see it through. If you can, it would be a help. We have enough trouble as it is," the Great Waffler went on, "and this would bring more three or four ways. Why are we sheltering the enemy of a friendly nation? Why are we assisting that enemy to rob that nation? Why are we refusing political asylum to a man—boy, really— whose greatest crime is to be the exiled ruler of a once-friendly state? Why——" The Great Waffler broke off, and waggled the same two fingers, wearily. "You see what I mean? Much better if Pat could see this through himself without having official intervention. We can sort it out afterwards, but——"

"We're on our way," said Ted. "Only one problem—which car to go in?"

## CHAPTER XIX

## THE VILLAGE

TED BERESFORD and Tim Jeremy walked away from the Great Waffler's car, looking and feeling very subdued. The police, who had recognized the great man, were obviously impressed; they actually saluted when Ted and Tim stopped at the Jaguar. Beresford put a hand on the roof, affectionately.

"I'll go the low road and you take the high road," he said, and hummed the words to the tune that anyone would recognize. "Seems best, I think, but we ought to have some kind of code."

"Could meet in the village," said Tim. "For that matter, we could go to the village first, see the lie of the land there, and then we could take the high and the lower roads. Wouldn't take any longer, and we might get some dope that would help. If you ask me," he added soberly, "we should both go through Haslemere, for a start. When we know what the village position is, we can have a look round nearer the house. Right?"

Ted nodded. "Right. I'll wait for you."

He didn't even grin.

Five minutes afterwards, the old yellow Bentley snorted past him on the by-pass, making enough noise to deafen three jet planes which were manœuvring overhead. Ted grinned, that time, but he wasn't in a mood for smiling much. He didn't think beyond what he had been told by the Great Waffler; and he tried not to worry too much about Dawlish. Dawlish had a way of getting out of hot spots, but this . . .

Ted kept his foot down.

He slowed down a little through Haslemere, but trod on it again towards Alum Village. Within a few hundred yards of Haslemere on the Alum side, he saw the first indications of an isolated village. There was a cottage, and outside the cottage a police car, four policemen, an old farm cart and some barrels.

The road was half-blocked; and it would take less than a minute to push the barrels into place and so block it in both directions. Two of the policemen, one of them on a bicycle, moved forward as Ted appeared, but then stood back and waved him on.

"Pass, friend," he said aloud.

At the next crossroads, he found a similar barricade and again he was waved on.

The next was a fork road, one turning going towards Alum, another wandering off across the Surrey countryside. Both roads were half-blocked, and this time he was stopped.

"It's Mr. Beresford, sir, isn't it?" a policeman asked.

"Yes. How are we doing?"

"Can't say that I know much about what's happening, sir," said the policeman, "but I know all roads leading to and from Alum are blocked."

"All?"

"Yes, sir. No one's allowed in. People who live there can come out, mind you, but they're not allowed to go back without permission. Would you mind showing me some kind of identification, sir?"

Ted produced a driving licence and his membership ticket of the Carilon Club.

"Quite all right, sir, thank you."

"Mr. Jeremy gone by?"

"Mr. Who? Jer—oh, in that old Bentley!" The policeman grinned. "Yes, 'bout five minutes ago."

"Could be worse," said Ted, as if to himself. "Could be a lot worse."

He drove on along a winding road. He knew it well. There were no more turnings to Alum, except lanes and bridle paths —and when he passed one of the bridle paths, he saw a solitary policeman by it, his bicycle against a hedge, his cape streaming with the rain. Ted waved. A hundred yards further on, he saw the first houses of the village; and here was another barricade and, not far beyond it, the old Bentley.

They let him pass.

Tim, several policemen, and a little, subdued man whom

Ted knew from previous visits, were gathered together under the covered porchway of The Bull, the door of which was wide open. A few villagers, wearing raincoats and knee-boots, were standing around. At every window, one or two people watched. A single-decker bus was parked in the yard of The Bull, and a dozen people were sitting in it, while the conductor argued with a policeman.

Ted left the Jaguar and went to the porch.

"Hi," he said, and waited.

Tim didn't keep him long, and introduced a harassed, wiry man as Dawlish's neighbour, Robert Marsh.

"Not a lot happened since we were told about it," Tim went on. "The only certain thing is that no one will be able to get away from Four Ways. Had one or two chaps on the look-out," he added, "up trees and things. Several men are in the grounds up there, two armed for certain. Guards. Fel's car is parked on the drive, to make sure that no one can go the quick way in. Guards at the gates. We could send a raiding party which would climb the walls and hedges, of course, but not a real hope of catching anybody by surprise until after dark. And then . . ."

For Tim, he was glum.

Bob Marsh said slowly, wearily: "I didn't think I'd ever live to see the day when a thing like this happened. The police seem *frightened*! It's as if——"

"Tactics," Tim said quietly. "Simple fact seems to be this, Ted. Pat got in, Fel's there, and the pair of them are unable to get away. Six or seven men in the house, and they've shown that they mean business by killing Hal Scott. You knew Hal."

"Why don't you rush the place?" Marsh demanded harshly. "Why have you just blocked all the roads off and made it impossible for anyone to get in or out? If you wait until dark, they might be killed."

"Tactics," repeated Tim. "Save bloodshed, if we can, and it looks quite as serious as that. Ted, we'd better get on. You take the low road and I'll take the high road. And you wait——"

Ted interrupted: "We'll toss up for it and no arguing.

Whoever takes the high road—that's the one from your farm,
Mr. Marsh—will wait just at the top of the slope, and see what
happens when the other one goes in." He took a coin from his
pocket, and tossed it high.

"Heads," Tim called.

It was heads.

He smiled faintly. "You take the high road. You can keep
a good look out from there. I'll get inside the house if I can.
Give me twenty minutes or so. If I'm able to get in and out,
I'll raise both arms, skywards; meaning don't come, because
Pat and I can manage. Or I won't raise my arms—in which
case come as fast as the devil drives."

A police inspector said: "We'll have a radio-car standing
by with Mr. Beresford, and can order a general raid at short
notice. If you don't signal, we'll close in."

Tim nodded.

"Right" he said. "I'll just drive up to the house as if I
didn't know that anything was the matter. Should be able to
fool 'em. Er—I was told that you people here would have all
the usual weapons of war and things. Such as tear-gas."

The police inspector said uneasily, "Yes, sir and we've
had instructions to allow you to do what you think best, but
in my opinion——"

"You're almost certainly right, too," said Tim. "The
trouble is that Dawlish and the pair of us have worked a lot
together." He took a small automatic from the inspector's
hand, and squinted down the barrel, like any fool. "How many
tear-gas pellets?"

"A dozen."

"Refills?"

"We won't want any refills," Ted said, and took a second
gun. "Thanks. If you haven't fixed it with a dozen shots, I'll
come and get you out of the mess."

"You're off-form," Tim said. "They could cobble my gun,
but if I had a few spare capsules—as Pat would put it, I'd be
thrice armed." He was quite straight-faced, and the policemen
nearby looked shaken and horrified. "If only we could get one
of the beggars, and find out a little of what's going on——"

He broke off.

Marsh gave a funny kind of strangled cry. The inspector handed over some tear-gas pellets. They looked towards the Vauxhall, which was drawn up into the car park. A small boy, with a raincoat draped over his head, was peering inside. The policemen, Tim and Ted looked from the farmer to the Vauxhall and back again.

"He won't hurt it," said Tim, gently.

"Yours?" asked Ted.

"In—in the boot, Dawlish said there was a man in the boot," Marsh cried. "I completely forgot!" He was wearing only his tweed jacket and the old hat, but plunged into the teeming rain, getting wet through before he reached the car, but snatching the keys from his pocket as he ran. Fast as he went Tim drew level with him, and Ted wasn't far behind nor were the policemen.

Marsh thrust the key into the lock.

"If he was right——" he began hoarsely, and lifted.

He broke off.

There was the tall, thin-faced man, on his back, with his knees bent and poking upwards. He was looking at them with startled, frightened eyes. For a moment, Marsh and the others did nothing, were too taken aback even to speak. Ted, bringing up the rear after all, broke the short, sharp silence.

"Pity," he said heavily.

"Wha—what do you mean?" Marsh demanded. "Wha——"

"I mean, it's a pity we've so many spectators," announced Ted Beresford, and his face was set very hard, there was nothing even remotely genial about him. He shouldered Marsh aside, and the great arms shot out. Webber tried to cringe away but Beresford gripped him by the waist, yanked him out, and held him upright.

He began to shake him.

The police, the watching villagers, the people in the bus, everyone in sight, stared with growing astonishment, for Webber wasn't a small man. Yet Beresford didn't slacken his grip or the fury of his shaking. Webber's head jolted to and fro, his mouth opened and closed, he kept trying to open his eyes, but they only fluttered. Two people called out, "Stop it!" but Beresford took no notice. In fact the performance lasted only thirty seconds; to everyone watching it seemed more like half an hour.

Then, Beresford lowered the man.

Had he let him go, Webber would have fallen. Instead, he was held upright, staring into Ted's face and seeing one, as hard and unrelenting, beside it; Tim's. The police kept out of it, deliberately.

At last, Beresford said, "What are they doing up there?"

Webber didn't try to hold out or to argue. His head hung limply. He was still wholly dependent on Beresford's support. He started to speak, but at first could only manage a kind of gibberish, but gradually the words took on an intelligible sound.

"They—they won't let themselves be caught alive, they'll kill themselves. *They won't be caught alive.*" He kept saying the same thing over and over again. "I'm sure of it, they won't be caught alive!"

"Listen," said Beresford, and Webber stopped on the instant, terrified lest that awful shaking should start again. "We want to get in. How——"

"They won't let you get in," Webber gabbled, "they won't let you get in, they'll make sure they're not caught alive. If they'd been able to get away unseen it would have been all right, but——"

He broke off.

Ted said, very quietly: "We'd better get off, Tim. Got to get in there somehow, and obviously a crowd's no good. See what the old boy meant, now." He rubbed his big, fleshy chin. "You're taking the low road, aren't you?"

"Low, yes," said Tim, firmly. "I take first shot, you just cover me." He smiled. "Remember?"

"Never had much time for you and your double-headed pennies," said Beresford, although everyone there knew that he had taken a coin out of his own pocket. "All right. Nothing beats trying," he added earnestly, and looked round at all the men assembled, "but doing," he finished. "Ready, Tim?"

They went to their cars, while the police took charge of Webber.

.    .    .    .    .

"It's madness," Bob Marsh gasped, "they'll be slaughtered, the only way to get into Four Ways is in force. Is everyone crazy?"

No one answered; unless the harsh beat of the old Jaguar and the roar of the vintage Bentley answered him.

.    .    .    .    .

Tim Jeremy, taking the low road past the crossroads and the trees where Dawlish had hidden before the capture of Webber, slowed down only a little before he took the corner. Normally he would now roar the engine so that Dawlish and Felicity would not even have to look out of the window to see who it was; only one car in all the world made such a noise as that. Then, he would take a wide swing, hoot powerfully and turn into the gates, but his foot would be ready for his brake.

It was, now.

He knew that the drive was blocked, but he had to pretend that he didn't, for if he was simply travelling to see Dawlish, why should he have been warned?

He pressed his horn.

He turned, saw the Californian in front of him, and jammed on his brakes as if he was utterly astounded. He glanced up, saw Dawlish at the window, and believed that he also saw Felicity.

There was no one else.

He stopped the Bentley only a foot in front of the Californian, and the engine stalled. He didn't get out at first, but sat gaping. He knew that he could be seen by several of the guards, but behaved as if no one at all was watching him.

Explosively, he said, "Well, hell's bells!"

He opened his door and got out. Rain swept over him, but no one was in sight. He squeezed past the Californian and

looked at the house, the door of which was closed, now. Then
he began to walk towards it. He didn't know whether they
would let him go far and he didn't know whether, if they shot
at him, they would shoot to kill.

There was just one way to find out.

CHAPTER XX

. . . MY PARLOUR

HANNA OF GOETZ had said very little for the past five
minutes, but she had lost much of her calm and her poise. By
contrast, Felicity was now cool and detached. Dawlish left
them together, while he prowled round the room. He knew
exactly what he wanted to do, simply wasn't sure that there
was any way to do it in time.

Felicity said, "What are you looking for, Pat?"

He looked round at her from the open wardrobe.

"A screwdriver, claw-hammer and a cold chisel would do,"
he said brightly. "I'd settle for the screwdriver." He rummaged
inside the wardrobe. "Used to be a bed-key in here, that might
do. Would help, anyway."

"What do you want it for?"

"Tricks," said Dawlish.

Felicity looked at him with her head on one side, and there
was a smile in her green-grey eyes, as well as a touch of
moisture. She sounded choky when she said:

"Bless you. But the bed-keys are in the spare room."

"Oh, lor'," said Dawlish lugubriously. "Well, they probably wouldn't have done, anyhow! Why I didn't shove a
screwdriver into my pocket before I came I don't know. I'm
slipping, and——"

Hanna whirled round on him.

"Why are you talking like this? What is funny?" She
clenched her fists and took a pace towards him. "Why do you

not believe what I say to you? If you do not give me a chance he will destroy us *all*."

"You know, I think he'll leave it as long as he can," said Dawlish, mildly, "and——"

He stopped, and turned towards the window.

A new sound had penetrated—the deep, baying roar of a car engine. He took three swift strides towards the window, pulled the curtain back an inch at one side, and stared out. Felicity went towards him, almost as quickly. The baying note was louder, and getting still louder and nearer every second. Dawlish's expression was taut and bleak, yet there was a smile in his eyes.

Felicity was gripping his arm.

"That's Tim," she said.

"Yes, my sweet," agreed Dawlish softly, "that's our Tim. And Ted won't be far away." He looked beyond the wall and the meadow, and, just visible in the misty, November-like gloom, there was a stationary car. "My shirt's on that for Ted's Jag," he said.

Then, they saw the yellow monster swing into the drive.

"He'll crash!" Felicity exclaimed. "Pat, stop him, tell him to go back, if they get him——"

She broke off.

There was no time to shout a warning to Tim Jeremy about the Californian; he must have seen it already. The old Bentley seemed to leap into the air and then land on all four wheels, quivering like a horse which had shied at a fence.

"Open the window, send him away," Felicity said tensely. "He just hasn't a chance——"

Dawlish said, "It's a time for taking chances, my sweet." He watched as Tim climbed out of the car, looked at the Californian as if shocked, and then glanced at the house; he must have seen Dawlish and Felicity, but he gave no sign. He squeezed between Felicity's car and the bank, dusting his hands on the side of his trousers. He wore an old and battered trilby, his raincoat looked saturated, and he seemed too thin to stand alone.

No one was in the grounds now.

For the first time everyone was out of sight.

"They're letting him come in," Felicity breathed. "Pat, what's the matter with you, why don't you send him away?"

"He prefers to walk into the parlour," said Dawlish. He felt Felicity try to move away from him, but he held her tightly, and for the first time since he had arrived, he said: "I'll get you out of it, and as soon as we can get that arm fixed, we will. Is it too bad?"

"It—it aches a bit."

"Nice understatement," said Dawlish. "We ought——"

"Pat," said Felicity, and there was a note of distress in her voice, "I simply don't understand you. Why don't you stop Tim before they catch him?"

"Tim knows what he's doing," Dawlish assured her, and dropped his voice. "Think Hanna does?"

Felicity started.

They turned their heads—and saw Hanna pushing at the bedstead which had been tight against the door. The other, which had jammed the door, was leaning to one side, and in another minute, perhaps less, she would have been able to get the door open. When she saw Dawlish, she made a despairing effort to pull the bed away but it was too heavy for her, and she had to stop.

"Get away from me," she ordered fiercely. "Don't come near me! I am going out."

Felicity exclaimed, "Pat!"

For Hanna, pressed close against the wall, snatched an automatic pistol from the bed. She'd put it there so that she could get at it quickly, must have had it hidden all the time she had been here. Now, she covered Dawlish and Felicity, and in the bright grey eyes there was a desperate, feverish look.

"I am going to talk to Otto," she went on. "Come and open the door for me."

Dawlish didn't move.

Except for Hanna's breathing and the steady tread of

Tim's feet on the gravel of the drive, there was silence; an ominous, heavy silence. On Felicity's face there was a look of horror—as if this were the last crushing straw, and she couldn't stand any more.

"*Open the door,*" Hanna repeated, and now her voice was husky, as if she couldn't speak clearly. "*Hurry.*"

"Where do you think this is going to get you?" Dawlish asked quietly. "Supposing you do get out——"

"*Open the door or I will shoot you!*"

"All right," said Dawlish, and his voice broke, he seemed to lose his self-control and all the strength which had kept him going. His voice wasn't even angry. "If you know what you're talking about he'll probably kill you as well as us. My way there might be a chance."

"Don't talk, just let me out!"

"All right, all right," said Dawlish. He was close to the side of the bed.

Hanna snapped, "Don't come too near me!"

He said, "Think I'm going to try conclusions with a mad woman who has a gun?" He put his great hands to the side of the bed. He could lift it and shift it away from the door, and Hanna could be outside in a flash. He actually started to move it to the right side, under cover of that gun; and then, before she realized what he was doing, before even Felicity guessed, he heaved the bed in the other direction, so that he banged against Hanna.

She staggered and her arm waved.

Dawlish leapt . . .

He looked at the little automatic, now in his great hand, and smiled broadly at her.

"Hanna," he said chidingly, "you shouldn't lose your head. People who lose their heads in a situation like this don't live long." He pushed the bed back into position and strengthened the barricade with the other bed, then handed the automatic to Felicity. "Look after this, sweet, will you?"

Felicity looked as if she were nearer swooning, but she took it.

Hanna was breathing hard; noisily.

"I am not going to stay here," she breathed, "I'm not——"
She darted towards the window.

Dawlish overtook her before she reached there, and gripped
her shoulders—and it was like trying to hold a wild cat. She
struggled and kicked and struck at him, and her eyes blazed
with fury, her lips were twisted, her teeth showed small and
white and perfect; he could see the tip of her tongue. He held
her very tightly, and at arm's length, so that she was scratch-
ing at the air and beating it hopelessly—and it seemed a long
time before she stopped.

Felicity was standing up.

Hanna seemed to collapse. Her body went limp and, as
Dawlish released her, she buried her face in her hands. Her
shoulders heaved. Dawlish smiled at her, one-sidedly. Felicity
moved to her, and led her to the larger of the easy chairs. Now
that the paroxysm had passed, Hanna seemed helpless and
hopeless; just a young girl who was facing death and didn't
seem to see any way out.

"I'll look after her," Felicity said reassuringly. They all
stood there for a moment, and Felicity and Dawlish were
listening to a rumble of voices downstairs; one voice was
raised and loud, and the tone was unmistakable.

"Tim's having plenty to say," Dawlish remarked.

Felicity didn't comment; now that it was over, she
wouldn't say a word, knowing that reproach was pointless;
yet he realized that she thought he had failed Tim.

Betrayed him?

He moved away from Felicity towards a corner near the
fireplace. Hanna was still crying, silently. Felicity helped her
into the chair. Dawlish shifted a small table and a chest of
drawers, and then pulled at the carpet in the corner. He had
an ordinary pen-knife, and used it to lever up the big tacks.
After a few seconds, he ripped several tacks out at once, and
a corner of the carpet was free from the floor. He pulled it
further, standing up now and heaving; it made a noise like a
thick cloth being ripped.

He rolled the carpet back, and then pulled the underfelt
and stared at the bare, unstained boards. Two of these had

been cut and screwed back into position, although most of them had been nailed.

He used the pen-knife on the screw-heads. Both were rusted. He broke the tip off one blade, and tried another. The tip snapped and flew into his face, and he closed his eyes. The sharp point stabbed at his cheek, drawing blood.

But the knife-blade was firmer here.

He worked on the first screw, until it began to move; and by then there was sweat on his face and forehead, and he kept wiping his chin. He started on the second screw; it was easier. The fourth, which was loose already; the fifth—which gave more trouble than the first.

Men were still talking downstairs.

Hanna was huddled in the chair, and Dawlish worked more swiftly. The screws came out, one by one. He lifted the length of floor-board, about three feet in all, and with that on one side, he tugged at the boards on either side. Nails groaned as he pulled them out of the joists.

Felicity was watching intently.

Hanna lifted her head.

Dawlish pulled another floor-board out, and started on a third, and this time when he pulled it free from the joists, it made a sharp report; almost as loud as a pistol-shot. He sat back on his haunches, listening. There was a break in the flow of conversation below, and he knew that even Tim had stopped talking.

Now Dawlish had to dislodge two of the joists. Once that was done, there was only the plaster between the bedroom and the morning-room below, plaster which he could break with his great fists.

The difficulty was to judge the right moment.

Now he could hear the voices much more clearly—Tim's, Otto's, occasionally another man's. Emil's?

.      .      .      .      .

Tim Jeremy sensed the watching eyes as he walked up the drive, but he obeyed as if he was just wet, miserable and even exasperated. He even had his hands in his pockets, and his shoulders were hunched. The closed door seemed like a barricade. He knew that Pat and Felicity were at the window but didn't look up at them.

He saw a man sheltered behind a corner of the house.

His heart turned over, but he didn't slacken pace and didn't miss a step.

He reached the porch.

His forehead was wet with rain and with his own sweat. His teeth were clenched, now. If they were going to shoot, this would be the most likely time, when he was close enough to make an easy target, and before he got into the house. And one shot could kill, remember.

The door opened.

Tim caught his breath, but he didn't lose nerve. He actually scowled, took his hands from his pockets, and said in a deep and irritated voice:

"What's the great idea? Fel's car on the drive, I nearly broke——"

He stopped, as if stupefied, at the sight of Emil, who carried a gun. He gaped at the man behind Emil—and then heard a footstep behind him, glanced round, and saw the man from the corner.

He had both his hands in sight.

He gulped.

"I say," he said, in what seemed a startled voice, "must be some mistake. Called at the wrong house. Age, I suppose. Oh, *lor'*." He looked at fat Emil and his gun, and edged back. "You know," he said earnestly, "you ought to be careful. You——"

The man from the garden stepped on to the porch. Tim had never been frisked with greater speed or efficiency. The teargas gun changed hands; so did his pen-knife and his cigarette-case.

But not the spare pellets, which looked like tiny containers of lighter fuel.

He licked his lips.

"I protest," he declared hoarsely. "It's an outrage."

"You had better come in; you can protest inside," said Emil. He wasn't smiling at all, his voice was harsh, and the gun in his hand was very steady. "Do exactly what I tell you. *Exactly.*"

Tim stepped inside.

## CHAPTER XXI

### FIRE?

THE little man with the wrinkled face was in the drawing-room, standing by the fireplace and watching Tim as he came in, with Emil and one other man behind him. Tim put his head on one side, as he studied the lined face and the deep furrows in the forehead. This man had no gun, no weapon of any kind, and when he spoke his voice was quite flat and expressionless; yet, in a way, he frightened Tim more than did the fat man.

Otto said, "Are you a friend of Major Dawlish?"

Tim gulped. "Well—er—yes. Pals for years. Battle scars and all that to share you know."

"Did he send for you?"

Tim put his head on one side.

"Eh?"

Emil said heavily: "He seems to think that the situation is funny, Otto. I could suggest a way to make him take it more seriously."

Tim turned his head and said reproachfully: "If you knew how my heart was pitter-pattering, you wouldn't say that. Never been so scared in my life. First of all the car in the drive. Thought Fel must have gone crazy, leaving it there— why, I might have broken my neck! And now all this—what *is* going on?" he demanded, and then as if with a burst of inspiration: "And where's Pat? Dawlish, I mean. And Felicity —that's his wife. Where—*and what the hell are you all doing here?*"

"Did Dawlish send for you?" asked Otto, flatly.

"Otto," said Emil, "there is a good way to make sure that he talks. A little pain——"

Tim put his head on the other side.

"Between you and me, Otto," he said earnestly, "I don't like your fat friend, he has nasty ideas." He paused for a moment, and then decided that a little of the truth might go a long way. "Yes," he added.

"Dawlish did send for you?" Otto asked sharply.

"He did. Had a message this morning. Some kind of trouble, I gathered, and would I come and lend a hand? Well, what are hands for? Got the message a bit late, or I would've been here an hour ago—nearly tore the guts out of the yellow devil as it was. Last thing I expected was—damn it, the show must be over!"

Otto was smiling faintly.

"Very nearly over," he agreed. "Did Dawlish send for anyone else?"

Tim hesitated.

"*Did he?*"

"Between you and me, yes," said Tim, and licked his lips again, "but I don't think there's much to worry about with Ted. Nice chap and all that but he has a wooden leg—well, the modern equivalent, don't they make 'em of aluminium? —and that car of his just won't go. Passed it on the road surrounded by a flock of mechanics, road scouts, small boys and antiquarians, it——"

"Who was this other man?"

"Who? Oh, Ted. Ted Beresford. B-E——"

"A policeman?"

Tim shook his head, slowly and sorrowfully, and looked thoroughly unhappy.

"Fact is, no," he said, "that's the one trouble at times like these. All right if everything goes all right, of course, but if it doesn't, Bob's your uncle. I mean, what wouldn't I give to think that there was a nice bodyguard of cops coming up the drive. However, Pat said no cops."

"He *ordered* that?"

"If this man is lying——" Emil began.

Tim shot him a look of acute dislike.

"I still don't like your choice in friends," he said to Otto, earnestly. "Pat won't call in the police until the last minute, and I don't think he could have reached it. Didn't think he had, anyhow. No, since you've cornered me like this, collared my gun and all, there isn't much point in lying, is there?" He shrugged and looked really upset. "He had a friend in the village, an old farmer pal. Bob Marsh. Know Bob? Not like a farmer, really, cheerful kind of chappie! He was waiting for me in the village. Pat had copped someone from here, lanky lad with a doleful face and a semi-Roman nose, if you can follow me, and he said that there was some kind of a shindig up here, and I——Trouble is," Tim broke off, and he sounded quite forlorn, "in my youth I worshipped heroes, and I still try to be one. If I'd had any sense at all I would have called Field Marshal Montgomery for reinforcements, but I thought I could show Pat what it was like to have a friend who had the strength of ten. By the way—where *is* Pat?"

"Upstairs," Otto said, very deliberately.

"Not hurt, or anything like that?"

"No, not hurt," said Otto. "Not yet. He will be, soon, if he does not do what I tell him to do. I think he might listen to you." The suggestion came out almost casually, and Otto glanced at Emil, as if for approval. "It is really very simple. Mrs. Dawlish has some papers which His Highness gave to her, and in return for them I will allow Dawlish and his wife and *you*, of course, to go free. You will go and tell Dawlish that unless he produces those papers quickly—shall I say in five minutes from the time you speak to him?—I shall set fire to the house."

There was a pause. Then:

"Oh, *no*," breathed Tim.

"I shall set fire to the house," Otto insisted, "and I can do it without difficulty. I have here"—he motioned to a brief-case which stood by the side of an easy chair—"an incendiary bomb which would set the house on fire in . . " He paused and shrugged his immaculate shoulders and said, "In a few seconds at most."

He went to the case, unlocked it, and took out a tube of metal, one tightly packed with cotton wool. He pulled the wool away, then drew out a small, black cylindrical object, like a very fat cigar.

"If that is thrown, even if it is dropped lightly, it will explode, and—have *you* seen the effect of modern incendiary bombs?"

Tim said gruffly, "Yes."

"Then you know just what I mean," Otto said. "We should, of course, have men outside to make sure that Dawlish cannot escape from the window, and——"

Emil broke in, "We should start the fire in this room, immediately below Dawlish."

"*And* his wife," Otto said.

Tim, looking from one to the other, rubbed his bony jaw, and then slowly shook his head.

"Bloodthirsty couple of baskets, aren't you?" he observed flatly. "I'd like to crack your noisome heads together. Still, possession's nine points of the law. What's in these documents?"

"That does not concern you."

Tim kept rubbing his chin.

"Of course, one of the troubles is that you don't know Pat," he said. "Confront the great Patrick with an ultimatum like this, and he's inclined to put a finger to his nose. Wrong school, of course, but who can blame him? He——"

He broke off.

There was a noise above their heads which made all of them stare upwards. First, a sharp crack of sound, and then a kind of groaning. Otto looked alarmed, a man at the door looked in and said something in a language which Tim didn't understand.

Then, the noise stopped.

"I think it is time for you to go," said Otto, bluntly. "But before you do, you are to understand one thing. I am *quite* serious. I shall not allow anyone in this house to escape alive unless I get the documents. You will go and tell Dawlish that. And you will be watched, you will not have a chance to get into the room with him. I think it would be as well for you to understand that I do not care whether you live or die. I simply want those papers."

.        .        .        .        .

Tim thought, 'He means it.'

As he went slowly up the stairs, followed by one of the other men, he had a strange, cold feeling. That this was 'it'— and that Pat had bitten off more than he could chew. The deadliest danger came from Otto, who was so cold, calculating and completely free from any emotion.

A fanatic.

'Yes,' Tim thought, 'he means it. And he could set the place on fire, too.'

.        .        .        .        .

Otto and Emil stood close together at the foot of the stairs, watching Tim Jeremy. Two of their men were on the half-landing, each covering Tim. He hadn't a chance to go one way or the other, he had to do exactly what he was told.

Otto spoke in the Slavonic dialect of Goetz.

He said: "If we can get the documents now, Emil, we shall kill them all and then try to get away. When darkness comes, we have a chance. If we cannot get the documents——"

"We shall keep trying," Emil said.

Very slowly, Otto shook his head.

"There will be very little time," he protested. "I am not satisfied with this man's story, and I believe that the police are already in the village. If they are not, where *is* Webber? They are waiting because they do not want harm to befall Dawlish, and this man, his friend who pretends to be such a fool, is trying to find a way of setting Dawlish free. We have very little time, Emil, before the police come, and—it remains as it was before, we shall not allow ourselves to be caught. I know myself. I would much rather die. At least, we shall have tried."

Emil didn't speak.

Tim reached the landing, still with that cold eerie feeling and the sense of impending disaster; that it didn't matter what he said or what Dawlish did, they wouldn't get away.

Otto's cold, expressionless eyes seemed to be following him everywhere.

He reached the door.

He called, "Pat, are you there?"

.     .     .     .     .

"Pat," came Tim Jeremy's voice, "are you there?"

Dawlish was standing by the hole he had made in the floor now. He had heard the slow, deliberate approach from the stairs but hadn't appeared to take much notice. Now, he saw Felicity's head move up, and Hanna raise her head to look towards the door.

"Pat," Tim called again, "are you there?"

"Hallo, Tim." Dawlish moved across the room. "Sorry you bought it."

"Cash down, old boy, don't blame anyone but the customer. Pat, some unpalatable facts. The man Otto is serious."

"I gathered that."

"There's some document or other which Felicity snaffled."

"Yes."

"If you don't cough up, he'll burn the place down. Sorry. I'm quite sure that he means it. He has some kind of fire-raising stuff which he says will have it aflame in a matter of minutes, and I'm inclined to believe that, too. Saw an experiment. The sensible thing is to admit that you've had it, and hand over. I hate saying it."

There was a pause.

"Tim," said Dawlish.

"I'm still here, old boy."

"Go and tell Otto that two of us can be serious, will you?" asked Dawlish, distinctly. "Tell him that his Hanna is up here with us. Burn us, burn her."

Tim asked in a hollow voice, "*Who* did you say?"

"Hanna," repeated Dawlish firmly. "Tell Otto that if he wants Hanna, he must let us all go. It's as simple as that."

Tim said dubiously: "Well, I'll try. I don't know that I'm optimistic about it."

From the chair, Hanna said in a tired, hopeless voice:

"It will make no difference to Otto, he does not care what happens to me unless he has the papers. Why don't you believe what you are told? He will not allow you to stay alive, unless he gets those papers. Perhaps I could have helped you, but now——" She broke off, and she sounded as if she was quite sure that there was no hope at all. Then, fiercely: "Let me go to him! I could still try!"

Dawlish didn't answer her.

"That the lot?" Tim asked.

"One other little thing," said Dawlish. "Be careful of Emil. I don't trust Emil at all."

"I know what you mean," Tim said, and turned away.

Dawlish watched the door.

Hanna stood up for the first time since her outburst, and went across to the window. This time, Dawlish hadn't tried to stop her, it no longer mattered whether she was seen or not. The lights were out, and the room was dark even when she pulled the blinds back. Dawlish glanced at the light switch, but decided to leave it.

All was quiet, now.

He had the same kind of feeling as Tim; as Hanna; as Felicity. The chance was very slim. Get through that hole in the floor and into the drawing-room, but—getting out of there would be almost as dangerous as getting out of here. The one chance would come from the surprise.

"And there is Josef, too. Josef, who began all this!" Hanna said, fiercely again. "Why don't you let me try?"

* * * * *

Prince Josef of Goetz still lay on the door which had been turned into a table.

For the past hour he had been awake; not alert for much

of the time, but vaguely aware of what had been going on around him. Occasionally, someone came into the room to look at him, but he kept his eyes closed, and no one knew that he was awake. At that time, he was drowsy and did not want to be disturbed; he did not remember what had happened, just knew that he had a pain in his body, and that his head felt heavy and light at the same time.

Gradually, he grew more alert.

He not only heard men talking, but could understand what they said.

He heard shouting and running and banging; then, a period of quiet; next a sound as if an aeroplane was flying low and a disturbance in the hall.

Not long afterwards, he knew that men were going upstairs and, in the quiet of the house, he heard Otto speaking to Emil.

For the first time since he had come round, he began to think clearly, began to understand what was happening.

CHAPTER XXII

## JOSEF

JOSEF lay very still.

No one was in the room with him, and the house was quiet for a few moments, until Otto and Emil began to speak. What they said meant nothing to Tim, but a lot to the wounded prince. It was crystal clear that they intended to kill other people in this house—in Dawlish's house. Otto had made that all too clear.

They were to try to get the documents from Dawlish's wife, and if they succeeded, then Emil and Otto would leave and try to fight their way past any opposition so that they could collect the fortune; so that they could plot and plan their revolt again.

Revolt, purges, bloodshed.

Josef raised his head.

The talking had stopped, but he could hear a man speaking in English, although he could not make out the words. He was a long way off.

Josef moved his legs a little.

There was the pain at his stomach, and he knew what had caused it: the wound, when he had been shot. He could remember the ordeal of walking towards Dawlish's house, but that was behind him.

They talked of fire; and he knew of Otto's weapon.

He tried to sit up, but the pain at his waist was too great and he dropped back again, gasping. After that, the pain grew worse and the wound seemed to become hot, but Josef knew that he couldn't stay there.

The Englishman was still talking.

Josef eased himself over to one side, gripping the edge of the door which served as a table. He bit his bottom lip against the pain. Gradually, he rolled over until he was lying on his side, but now the fury of his aching head made him lie still, and the wound burned and streaks of pain came from it.

The man stopped talking. . . .

Then, Joseph shifted his legs, so that he could ease them off the table—trestles and door wedged so that they didn't move. He could see the floor, and it seemed yards, not feet, away. He knew what would happen if he fell, but he could not stay here and let this thing happen.

He edged one leg over.

He bit his lips until the blood showed.

He felt as if he would swoon, as if nothing could help him to stay on the table, but he didn't lose consciousness and he slid both legs off the table. Now, if he fell, he would not be able to get up.

*He must not fall.*

Somehow, he slid off the table until his feet touched the floor. The strain at his waist was almost unbearable, and he was groaning and gasping and sweating; but he didn't stop there for long.

Then, the Englishman spoke; next, Otto. Something about death and Hanna and Dawlish. Dawlish was trying to come to terms. As if Otto would come to terms with anyone or anything except—his country.

Josef knew Otto.

He stood away from the table, for the first time, swaying sideways, then swaying backwards and forwards, until at last he stood almost still. Pain was no longer only at his waist, it seemed to have spread over the whole of his body. Yet, he moved forward, to the door. It was ajar. He leaned against the wall while he pulled the door open.

He heard Otto say:

"You are to tell Dawlish that if he has not come out of that room five minutes from now, I shall set fire to the house."

'Fire,' echoed through the prince's head; and everything it meant. The door was as heavy as lead, and wouldn't open. He *had* to open it. He . . .

He pulled it open.

Gasping, he stepped into the hall.

He saw a tall man wearing a sodden raincoat, with a thin face and very bright brown eyes, starting up the stairs. Emil and Otto were not in sight, now, but two men were watching this Englishan; two men from Goetz.

Prince Josef couldn't speak, hadn't the strength now to move or raise his voice, just had to stay there, fighting to regain the little strength he needed so as to give orders. He *might* be obeyed.

Might.

He still leaned against the door jamb, watching the lean Englishman as he went slowly upstairs.

.     .     .     .     .

"Pat," Tim Jeremy called, clearly, "I don't think you've a chance in a hundred. This Otto chap doesn't care a damn what happens to Hanna. He says come out, or he'll start the fire. And I think he means it."

Dawlish said calmly: "Wouldn't be surprised. Tim——"

"Yes."

"Listen carefully. *Very* carefully. Could you manage a schemozzle for thirty seconds?" He paused, and then added with great care, *"Doh-Ray-Me-Fah-Soh."*

Tim was staring at the closed door.

Schemozzle was a word which these people probably didn't know; a row, a din, a hullabaloo. He didn't get it.

"What kind?" he asked.

Dawlish crooned, hopefully.

"Bellow and sing, as when tipsy!" For the first time since he had realized how deadly this threat was, Tim grinned. Then he thought of the grand piano in a corner of the drawing-room, over by the fireplace. *Doh-Ray-Me* ... A schemozzle! He didn't turn round and his voice was as flat and as glum as it had been before.

"I tell you that he means what he says. Five minutes isn't long."

"Thirty seconds would do."

"Can try," said Tim very softly, and then he went on: "If you take my advice, you'll give it up. Let the swab have those documents."

Hanna cried out shrilly, *"But he hasn't got them!"*

Her words carried clearly to the gunmen on the half-landing, and even to Emil and Otto. The gunmen repeated them in their own tongue. Emil swung round towards Otto, and flung them out again. Otto came swiftly and now his eyes were blazing; no one who had seen him before would have thought that such evil could come from him.

*"He hasn't got them!"* Hanna called shrilly, and then stopped, as if Dawlish had clamped a hand over her mouth.

"Who——" Otto began, and then stopped

Tim said, "Pat, they mean business," but he could only just get the words out. Dawlish wanted a distraction just for thirty seconds. The drawing-room by the grand piano was the best place. Never mind why a din was needed. Otto wanted to get those documents, and would have been prepared to talk but . . .

Dawlish *hadn't* got them.

Hanna had killed what hope there was of bluffing.

Tim said, "If that girl's lying, you'd better make it clear soon." He turned round and walked towards the stairs and the half-landing, but his path was barred by one of the gunmen. He called:

"Can't do it by the baby, have to be here."

He slid his right hand into his pocket, and drew out two of the little refills for the tear-gas gun. He dropped and trod on them, and the gas sprayed out; he felt it clutch at his eyes before he had moved another step.

One of the men shot him.

He felt the bullet pluck at his waist, and it nearly brought him down, but he managed to keep upright. He raced down the stairs. He heard the sharp report of another shot, and a powerful blow at his right shoulder. He had no doubt at all how deadly they were, and that they would shoot to kill. He bellowed, not in pain but to try to startle them, and then staggered down the last two stairs and tried to rush towards the open front door.

He believed he would be shot again.

Then, he heard a crash above his head.

He didn't know what it was, only knew that it was a distraction which made the men at the foot of the stairs swing round and stare towards the drawing-room; and it halted the gunmen. He almost fell down, hardly knew how to keep on his feet. He saw dust and debris falling from the ceiling of the drawing-room, spraying the baby grand. He saw Dawlish's feet dangling from the ceiling. He saw Dawlish drop into the room, and the next moment Dawlish was standing upright, stretching up for Felicity.

Who else?

And the tear-gas was biting at the eyes and nose and mouth of the men on the stairs.

Tim kept on his feet, dropped another pellet as he reached the porch, and flung another into a doorway where he saw a man. The cold air stung his face and the rain splashed him with a welcome coolness. He was like a drunk, but at least no one from the house was shooting at him, he still had a chance. And Ted Beresford would see what was happening, and would soon be on his way.

Ted . . .

Tim staggered, and almost fell. One of the guards who had been in the grounds was watching him, standing quite still and looking very tense. There was shouting from the house; bellowing and shooting.

Tim stood as still as he could.

The guard raised his gun.

Tim's legs crumpled up, and he dropped flat. The bullet passed over his head. The guard hesitated, then began to run towards the house.

The window of the drawing-room smashed, and a chair came hurtling through, struck the crazy paving of the path just outside, and broke. Glass splintered and then rattled. Tim lay there, unconscious. . . .

A long way off, Ted Beresford started the engine of his car; and a police radio began to send out its message. But the fastest car would take much longer than there was time to spare. There was the Californian on the drive, and Tim's car. Men who had to come on foot would take five minutes at least, ten or fifteen if they were opposed.

The afternoon was dark and the mist was like a shroud.

. . . . .

Dawlish kept his eyes narrowed against the falling dust and plaster, and stretched his arms up for his Felicity. He was like a man standing there with his arms raised in supplication to a god whose mercy he doubted. He could see Felicity as she scrambled over the edge of the hole he had made, and knew that she would throw herself down bodily, but—her slip caught on the edge of a joist.

He couldn't reach her.

She pulled desperately to free herself.

Tim had gained him the respite he needed. Once out of here with Felicity in his arms he would run with his whole future, and he did not give a thought to the gunmen there. But she couldn't free herself.

"Fel," he breathed.

He dropped his arms, grabbed the nearest chair, and hurled it at the window. It went right through. He picked up another and hurled that too, until the hole was large enough for him to step through. Then he climbed on to the piano. His knees slipped on the shiny surface. He couldn't stand easily, but he got to his feet, and now he could almost reach as high as Felicity's waist.

He lifted her, and lowered her.

Above, staring down, was Hanna.

And he had thought that girl was beautiful!

Almost choking, almost blinded, he scrambled with Felicity off the piano, and turned towards the window—and then he stopped quite still.

One of the guards was outside.

The man was crouching, and pointing his gun this way. Not far beyond him Tim lay in a crumpled heap. Afar off, there were noises; a car engine, roaring. In the house, there were raised voices and spluttering and coughing, and he could smell the tear-gas and sensed what Tim had done. That had given him his respite.

Then, he swung round.

A man appeared at the doorway, looking through the cloud of dust. *Emil*, with his eyes streaming with tears the gas had caused. He held a gun, and he raised it sharply, pointed it at Dawlish, and fired.

Felicity flinched.

There was no bark of a shot, no spurt of flame, but a cloud of vapour—and before he had recovered from that moment of surprise, Dawlish felt the tear-gas bite at his nose and his eyes. Tear-gas. Two using the same tactics. Dawlish was almost blinded already from the specks in his eyes, but this made them ten times worse. He heard Felicity coughing and he spluttered himself—and he wouldn't be able to carry her much longer.

He turned from the door.

He wasn't sure which way he was heading. He knew that there was the gunman in the window, and the fat Goetzan in the doorway, the gas blinding him and making him cry and gasp—and he felt as Tim had felt, twice that day: that this time there was no hope, and he would not survive.

He heard Emil's voice, close to his ear. He felt Felicity wrenched from his grasp. He heard another woman's voice: Hanna's. Left by herself, Hanna had pulled at those beds until she'd been able to open the door. Dawlish only just understood what they were saying.

"She told me she hadn't got it," Hanna said.

"But he had it here, he must have it!"

"If she has she lied to *him*."

"I'll make her talk," Emil said, savagely, "I'll make her talk if I have to——"

Then he stopped.

There was a strange hush, outside the room as well as inside, while the dust settled and the rain spattered and the car roared towards the house, not half a mile away now, and other cars converged on it, carrying twenty men and more ready to raid.

Otto said, "We cannot hope to escape now, for I can hear men coming."

He had the small cylinder in his right hand, held lightly and loosely. Slowly, he drew it out of its protective container.

CHAPTER XXIII

## COMMAND

DAWLISH could not see the little man, but he could understand. He heard Hanna say, gaspingly, "He will do it." He heard Emil speak roughly, in the Slavonic dialect, without knowing what the man meant.

But it wasn't Otto or Emil, Hanna or any of the gunmen, who spoke next, quietly, hoarsely, and yet with stunning effect.

"Otto," said a youth who was out of sight, "you will not throw that down."

Still Dawlish could not see.

He heard Felicity exclaim, and he heard Hanna say, "*Josef!*" That was all. He could understand the tension. He knew that Josef had been very close to death, and that they had all believed that he was unconscious in the morning-room, that he couldn't hope to get up, but——

"Otto," repeated Josef, "you will not throw that down."

Dawlish put his hands to his eyes, to try to clear them. When he looked again he could see, but through a shimmering kind of mist, as through a rain-spattered windscreen. Behind him in the window there was a guard, watching with as tense an interest as anyone. Emil and Hanna were close to Dawlish, and Emil still had a hand on Felicity's arm. The effect of the gas had almost gone now.

Otto stood just inside the room.

"Otto," said Prince Josef, from the door, "you will not throw that down. Come, please, and give it to me."

He leaned against the door, one arm raised and the hand gripping the door-frame. His right hand was pressed against his waist, and the bandages there were stained crimson. He looked like death, standing there, and his voice had a strange, penetrating quality.

"Otto," he said, "please bring that to me."

He was this man's ruler.

Outside, Ted Beresford's car was swinging into the drive, and to the sound of rain was added the humming of the other cars, some near, some far. It was like a fleet of aircraft, a long way off.

Emil whispered something, hoarsely.

Hanna said, "Yes, quickly."

Dawlish didn't notice what they did; he was held fast by the magnetism of the scene in front of him, by the awful sight of the youth standing there, commanding, although he looked as if he might fall dead at any moment.

"*Otto, bring that to me.*" The penetrating quality had gone; the youth had to force his voice, and it was barely audible.

So far Otto hadn't moved, either to obey or to disobey. His face was in profile towards Dawlish, who had no idea of the glitter in his eyes, and did not know the battle going on in his mind.

Then, Emil moved swiftly towards the window.

Dawlish glanced at him.

Hanna was in front of him. Emil was waving to the gunman telling him silently to move to one side, and the man moved. Hanna climbed through the hole which Dawlish had made in the glass, and Emil followed. Dawlish looked away from them, knowing what they were doing, not surprised and not really caring.

If disaster came now, it would come from Otto.

Prince Josef's lips worked.

"Otto . . ." he began, but he couldn't go on.

Dawlish was ten feet away from Otto, who stood with that devastating missile in his hand, out of its container. If it dropped, it would explode; if it exploded it would set the house on fire in the fraction of a second; there would be no chance for them. One all-consuming flash, which would first throw them off their feet and, as it did so, would shrivel them up.

Josef took his hand away from the door jamb, and, with the other hand still pressed against his wound, he began to move forward. His lips formed Otto's name and the command again, but no sound came. All the strength he had must go into the effort of moving.

Dawlish took a long stride forward.

If Otto saw him, if Otto sensed the threat from behind, what would he do? Defy the boy prince, or—give way? And if he gave way, what then? If he dropped the deadly thing, it would be as bad as if he hurled it to the floor.

Dawlish took another step forward.

"*Ot-to*," Prince Josef whispered.

Then Otto said in a strained voice:

"Highness, there is nothing more we can do. You cannot blame me for what has happened, you brought it upon yourself and you brought it upon Goetz. Make no mistake, there is no hope for any of us now, and——"

Josef formed his name, but did not make a sound.

Otto raised his hand to smash the awful thing upon the floor—and Dawlish leapt.

He caught the little man's wrist. He twisted, and the cylinder dropped. He snatched at it with his free hand, and with an awful horror in his mind, for if he lost it, if it slipped and fell . . .

He held it.

He did not see the prince fall. He saw Otto strike out but that didn't matter, the man was easy to fend off. Dawlish turned towards the broken window, and saw Ted Beresford squeezing between the high bank and the Californian, and staring towards him, and he heard the humming of the other cars. Heading for the gate in the wall on the other side of the drive were Hanna and Emil, running as fast as they could over the sodden grass and towards the open gate through which this horror had come a few short hours ago.

He didn't see Otto take a gun from his pocket.

"Pat!" cried Felicity. "Pat, *mind, mind!*"

He glanced round, to see Otto and his gun—and Felicity throwing herself at the little man. Otto fired. Dawlish felt no pain, but heard the bullet smash into glass near his head; slivers of glass sprayed over him.

He did not see the gunmen who had been in the hall, and who had stopped at Josef's command. He did not see Josef pitch forward, or these men rush towards him, to raise him up. He only saw the rain, Ted Beresford, the familiar grounds, now so murky and damp. He awkwardly stepped into the garden.

He hurled the cylinder towards the far side of the drive, over the hedge, and towards a lawn. It went smoothly, just a dark shape against the lowering sky. It disappeared, and as it went, he bellowed:

*"Down, Ted, down!"*

He flung himself on his face, and as he did so, heard the roar of the explosion, and felt the blast tear over him. The trees saved him from the worst although it was as if some savage hurricane had plucked at him and lifted him bodily and flung him a dozen yards away, He heard, after a moment of quiet, the smashing of windows and the falling of glass. He was helpless and breathless for what seemed an age, but there was desperate fear in his mind: that the blast might have hurt Felicity.

He tried to pick himself up.

He couldn't. . . .

He got to his knees, and then felt the heat from the burning. All the bushes and shrubs, the grass and the trees were on fire, the flames were shooting tens of feet into the air, making a holocaust. No man or creature could have lived in it for a single second.

The flames devoured the grass and everything near it, smoke rose like a grey pall—and the heat singed Dawlish's hair and eyebrows, and he had to close his eyes against it.

He got to his feet.

"Fel," he said in a constricted voice, and turned round.

The drawing-room windows had suffered less than most, for the blast had found its way in through the holes he had made. Every other window was out, and the house seemed filled with empty, blind eyes and with silence.

The fire was far behind him, now.

He reached the window.

Inside, Felicity lay in a heap, close to Otto, who was motionless on his back. A sliver of glass a foot long had struck Otto in the neck, and there were several pieces in his face and one very near his eyes. There was no hint of movement. He might be stunned, or might be dead—and as Dawlish went nearer he could have taken that thin neck between his fingers and squeezed out what life there was left in the man.

Felicity was face downwards.

He reached her, and turned her over, with a fierce gentleness.

She wasn't touched; except for pallor she was just as he had seen her last, and she was breathing.

Dawlish knelt there staring at her.

And Ted Beresford, running as fast as his artificial leg would allow, came on towards the house. He stopped at Tim, but didn't stay longer than to stare into his face and to judge that he was still alive. There would be others here, soon, the cars were already in the road nearby.

He wanted to find Dawlish, above all things.

He did not even give a thought to Emil and Hanna, who were near the gate in the wall.

.        .        .        .        .        .

As they reached the gate, Emil thrust the girl to one side, and went through first. He saw a police-car come through a gate in the field which bordered the road, and knew that there would be no escape that way. He turned towards the back of Four Ways, and Alum Farm, calling sharply to the girl. She caught him up. He held her arm tightly and helped her on, as police came towards them.

But the police were a long way off.

At the top of the field which ran alongside Dawlish's house, there was a view which showed many miles of countryside on a fine day; and even now, showed Alum Farm, nestling in a hollow, with smoke rising slowly from its chimneys. Emil turned towards it.

"If—there is a car——" He stopped, gasping, and Hanna made no response but kept going alongside him. "We can— search——"

Hanna said, suddenly, "It is a waste of time to run, we cannot get away."

She stopped.

Emil turned his head. "Hanna, come with me. Hurry!"

She said, "It is a waste of time." She put a hand to a pocket of the beautifully cut skirt, and took out a small metal phial. She pulled the tiny lid off this, and shook two white tablets on to the palm of her hand. "It was worth trying, but now it is useless," she said. "Too many men have been killed, and I do not want to be hanged. That would not be good for Goetz!" Her lips twisted in a bitter sneer, and she was breathing hard as she looked at the tablets. "May Josef of Goetz be damned for the rest of time! To think that fool would interfere, would stop us just when we were about to succeed. How we planned, you and I, how we fooled Otto into believing we had only the future of Goetz in our hearts!" The words almost choked her. "But for Josef we would have had everything, but now— Emil, take one of these before they catch us."

Emil was moving back towards her.

Five policemen, spread out in a line, were making what speed they could towards these two. Another car had come through the gateway and was heading across the field for Alum Farm, obviously to cut them off. Behind them rose the great pall of smoke, but not over the funeral pyre of men, only over land which would quickly recover and would grow again.

"Hanna, wait," Emil said desperately. "We can try to get away, and can still look for the jewels. *Hanna!* They will not hang us, not you and I, we are protected, we——"

She said sneeringly: "Are you *afraid* to die? The clever one, the brave one, who even made Otto believe that it was glorious to die for one's country, to plan the death of a thousand men—are you *frightened*, Emil?"

She raised the tablet to her lips.

"No!" he screamed, and leapt forward and struck her hand aside. The little tablet, looking so harmless, pressed against her lips, and melted, then hissed and fell on the wet ground. As it did so, a little hiss sounded, then came the faint smell of bitter almonds. "I shall not let you die," Emil shrieked at her. "They won't hang us, and Josef will die. The jewels will be ours; Goetz will be yours. What else have we worked and planned and plotted and killed for?"

Hanna said softly:

"We have plotted and killed so that I shall inherit the wealth of Goetz, and you and Otto shall take the blame."

## CHAPTER XXIV

## THE WEALTH OF GOETZ

EMIL stood staring at Hanna as if he could not believe a word she said. His mouth was open, gaping, less from horror than from shock. The police were approaching at a steady pace, but the mist was too thick for them to see anything in detail.

Emil gripped her arm.

"Hanna, what are you saying? You and I——"

"Not you and I," corrected Hanna, "there is nothing I wish to share with you." She was still sneering at him. "I would not trust you, Emil, any more than I would trust Otto or others. I worked with you because I wanted the fortune for my own use. But now—I *know* where the jewels are. I spoke just now to Josef. He trusted me, because he knew that he could not trust you or Otto. Poor, blind Emil! You schemed to get the wealth out of Goetz. You planned to get hold of it, when Otto had failed with his rebellion and was dead. You planned to share it with me, but—I *am* a princess of Goetz. With Josef dead it is all mine."

He said gaspingly, "You will tell me where it is, or——"

She turned, as if to run. He grabbed her. She put a hand against his mouth as if to force him away, and in her fingers was another tablet of cyanide. She pressed it against his lips and felt him gasp, heard the little hiss of breath as he drew in death. She kept her face averted and could not smell the gas.

Now the police came running, and the nearest was only thirty yards away.

Emil, with the acid biting his throat and choking him, let Hanna go and staggered away, making gasping, choking sounds, and she pretended to fall, as if she had no strength left. The first policeman was near enough to see the contortions on Emil's face, and to shout a warning:

"Watch him."

"What is——"

"Prussic acid, I think."

"You mean he——" began the second policeman to come up, and then he looked at Hanna as the first man helped her to her feet. She looked as if she had lost consciousness. "My hat," he said, "there's a looker for you! Is she all right?"

"She'll do," said the first policeman.

He lifted her, and carried her towards the house, where more police had arrived, all the men of Goetz had been disarmed, and where a doctor was already attending to Tim and to Josef. Soon, ambulances would be here. Four men were manhandling the Californian out of the way, taking it down the drive and into a wide stretch of road. Police patrols were passing up and down, there were road barriers approaching Four Ways but nowhere else.

.　　　.　　　.　　　.　　　.

Urgent messages were being sent to London; a telephone call reached the Great Waffler as Tim Jeremy and Prince Josef were being put gently into the ambulance.

He waggled his fingers.

"How about Dawlish?"

"He's all right," said the local Chief of Police.

"His wife?"

"She's wounded slightly," the Great Waffler was told, "but she isn't in any danger. She won't even need to go to hospital. Otto and Emil of Goetz are dead," the speaker went on, "Princess Hanna is alive."

"She all right?"

"Badly shocked," said the Police Chief, "but she should be all right when she's had some rest. Quite an escape, in her way, she . . ."

He went on, briskly; explaining.

In the same room, Dawlish was looking at a bullet, the nose flattened and the markings clear even to the naked eye, as he listened to the story. Thoughtfully, he took a gun out of his pocket; Hanna's .22. He raised it, taking aim at a thick wooden window-frame which was already badly damaged.

The report rang out, and the Chief of Police jumped round.

"What's *that*?" snapped the Great Waffler, into the telephone.

"Er—just an accident, sir, nothing really wrong," the policeman said, glowering at Dawlish.

Dawlish went to the window and, using a screwdriver, he had brought in from the garage, he began to prise the bullet out. It took him several minutes, and for the last two a police inspector watched him.

Dawlish got the bullet out, stepped to the piano and brushed a patch with his elbow. Dust billowed about.

"Sorry," he said, then placed both bullets side by side. "Happen to have a magnifying glass, Inspector?"

"Yes." The local man took one from his pocket.

Dawlish waved to the bullets.

"Help yourself," he said.

The superintendent kept on talking into the telephone as the inspector peered at the two bullets, which were the same calibre. Then he picked one up and examined it more closely; did the same with the other.

"I'd need an expert's corroboration before saying it in court, but they came from the same gun," he said. "Is that" —he pointed—"from Prince Josef's body?"

"On the mantelpiece in the room where he's been, anyhow."

Ted Beresford was sprawled out in a great armchair during all this. By his side was a large glass, in which a little whisky and soda was left. Outside the room men were moving about briskly, and upstairs Felicity was with a nurse and Hanna, who had come round soon after she had been brought back to the house.

Dawlish listened to the Chief, explaining about Hanna.

". . . she was playing a double game, sir, hoping to save the prince from any trouble. Apparently this Emil was sheltering behind Otto—Otto was the genuine fanatic. Emil wanted the stuff for himself. The princess knew that, and warned Josef, she says. Just before he collapsed, he told her where to find the papers which showed where the store is to be found. Somewhere in North Africa, but I haven't gone into full details yet, sir."

Dawlish had his head on one side as he watched and listened.

"Will the prince come round? Shouldn't think there's a lot of hope, sir, but I can't be sure . . . Yes, I'll keep you posted. Yes, I—hold on a minute, sir, please, Mr. Dawlish would like a word with you."

Dawlish was waving.

He strolled over, beamed, and took the telephone from the policeman's hand.

"Thanks. Hallo, cousin," he said mildly. "Ted's been telling me what a guardian angel you were. Thanks. As reward, I shall never accept any official position you offer me, for fear it would ruin your reputation."

The Great Waffler chuckled.

"I've come to believe it."

"My trouble is a suspicious mind, of course," said Dawlish, and he seemed to be smiling at the ceiling. "A very suspicious mind, especially about princesses in exile."

"Now what are you driving at?"—gruffly.

"Tell you in half an hour or so," Dawlish said. " 'Bye. And when I say thanks, that's exactly what I mean. Thanks."

"Here, Pat!" cried the Great Waffler.

But Dawlish had put the receiver down. He was looking at the puzzled Chief of Police, and out of the door. He thought he could hear Felicity's voice, but wasn't sure. He could certainly hear the doctor's, and he moved slowly towards the open door, where the doctor was attending a Goetzan who had been cut by flying glass.

"Doctor," he said.

"Won't be a jiffy."

"No hurry." Dawlish watched, and then looked up the stairs. Yes, Felicity was coming down. She wore the same cardigan with one sleeve hanging loose, but she looked a different woman. It was only an hour since she had fought with Otto to stop him from shooting Dawlish, but now she was as calm and as fair as a young bride; and she looked at

Dawlish as, a bride, she had looked at him so long ago. He stood, massive and solid and completely self-controlled.

"How's Hanna?"

"Oh, she'll be all right," said Felicity briskly. "I'm not at all worried about her. She's lying down, and I'm going to make her a cup of tea."

Dawlish gave his lazy smile.

"Correction," he said. "You're going to make her a *nice* cup of tea. Me, too, please."

Felicity went towards the kitchen and that part of the house which had hardly been touched. Dawlish saw her disappearing as the doctor looked up from the injured man. He was a younger doctor than Hal Scott, working in the same partnership, and he had lost both a friend and a mentor. When he stood up his expression had the hardness of grief.

"Now, what's your trouble, Mr. Dawlish?"

"About Josef," said Dawlish. "What are his chances?"

The doctor said: "It's hard to say. Fifty-fifty, at best. I think he would have been all right if he hadn't got off that bench and—but then, it's no use talking about that, is it?"

"Fifty-fifty?"

"Yes."

"Will he come round to talk?"

"I should think he will," said the doctor.

"Hm," said Dawlish. "Thanks." He went slowly upstairs, to the door of his bedroom. It was ajar. A policeman was in the bathroom, looking out of the window and shouting something to another man in the grounds. It was pitch dark outside, except where the darkness was broken by the beams of car headlamps.

He tapped at the bedroom door.

"Come in," called Hanna.

She was lying full length on Felicity's bed, the one near the window, and wearing one of Felicity's dressing-gowns. She looked very pale, and yet lovelier than she had except the moment when Dawlish had first seen her. When he stood looking down at her, she stared back—and gradually her expression changed, until she frowned. He still didn't speak.

She moved a little and, as he continued to look at her without speaking, she edged herself up until she was in a sitting position.

Felicity was at the foot of the stairs, saying something to the doctor.

"Why do you look at me like that?" asked Hanna, sharply. "Please go away."

"Me?" said Dawlish. "No, I won't go away, my pretty princess! I'm going to haunt you, far worse than any conscience. From now until the end of time, if necessary."

Dawlish heard Felicity exclaim, and then guessed that she compressed her lips tightly as she came up the second half of the stairs. The tea things rattled a little on the tray she was carrying with one hand.

"I don't understand you," Hanna said.

"I think you do," Dawlish told her, "and I'm sure you're going to. It was all very interesting and ingenious. Remember coming up and sneaking into the room when my wife was here, and pleading with *her* to let you have those documents?"

Hanna's eyes were cold; angry.

"I believed she had them. It was vital that no one should know I wanted them for myself. If Otto had suspected——"

"Trouble for the princess," said Dawlish, in his deep, rather drawling voice. "If Otto had known he would have taken your life first and worried about it afterwards. And if you'd got them, you would have killed Felicity and pretended an accident. You were so busy looking after Number One, Princess, that you didn't do a thing to help Josef. Or my friend Scott. Or my wife. And later, you cheerfully watched Emil die. I wonder if we'll ever know what happened to him."

"Are you mad?" Hanna cried.

"Not yet, Hanna," Dawlish said. "Of course, you had others in the plot with you. You weren't afraid of being seen at the window, because the guards knew you were here, and you were sure that you wouldn't be shot at. I don't suppose we'll ever find the whole truth, but there are some facts at hand. After all, right at the very end, you ran off with Emil.

Queer business. It was known that officially you'd all made a kind of multiple suicide pact, but you didn't keep it. You and Emil went off hell-for-leather. Then he's supposed to have tried to dose you with cyanide, as well as himself. *He* caught a packet, but——"

"I did not need to die," Hanna said, coldly.

"Pity," Dawlish went on, almost lazily. "Anyway, Emil died and you survived. Now, go back a little." He kept silent for a few seconds, watching her intently; and then he spoke with great deliberation. "What exactly did you do to Josef, Hanna? You shot him, of course, for the money and a useless throne, but—how? Who else knew?"

"It is not true!" she cried. "It is a lie!"

"If everything else was equal you would probably get away with that," said Dawlish. "The rest of the patriots dead, poor Josef a hallowed memory, and you a princess in exile sobbing on a fortune."

Hanna was breathing hard.

Felicity stood so quietly at the door that even the tea things were not rattling.

"But, Hanna," said Dawlish very softly, "you won't get away with it. I doubt if we'll ever know the full story, but several things have established themselves. You and the man Webber were expected here earlier. You were late. You had been in the chase. You had caught up with Josef. He didn't trust you at all, my pretty, but you shot him at close quarters, meaning to kill.

"Only—" Dawlish went on, softly, "Josef didn't die."

She cried: "He will die! He could never live——"

"He won't die," said Dawlish. "Lots of resistance, some of these young people. He's in hospital now, and he'll almost certainly be conscious before the night's out. A policeman will be sitting beside him, and the first question will be: *Who shot you?* Think he'll save your pretty face, Hanna?"

She was as white as the tablet with which she had killed Emil.

"I don't think he will," Dawlish said flatly. "I think he'll decide that the only safe thing will be to make sure that you hang for a part in the murders, or at least serve a long, long sentence for trying to kill him. Otherwise, you might try again, and succeed, and inherit.

"Mightn't you, Hanna?"

She screamed:

"But he won't live!"

"Oh, he'll live," said Dawlish, confidently. "And even if he were quixotic, we'd still have you on the spot. There was a gun that you pulled on me. I still have it. I fired a shot from it. The bullet is the same calibre, and under a magnifying glass has the same markings as the bullet which Hal Scott took out of Josef's body.

"And there's more.

"There was blood on the driving-seat in the Vauxhall, Hanna, the car you and Webber hired, the car in which you came to Alum. I'll never know exactly how it happened, but the shooting took place in the car. Josef got away. You went to the station to get the guards who, you believed, would serve you against Otto. Oh, it will sort itself out, though. When Webber is questioned and when Josef speaks——"

Hanna flung herself towards the window, as if to throw herself out, but he kept her back.

Outside, Felicity said wearily, "I suppose I'd better take this away, it'll be stewed."

.  .  .  .  .

Webber talked; and, two days later, Josef also told his story.

He had come to Alum by himself; Webber and Hanna had caught up with him, and forced him into the car. Otto and Emil had left the car to watch Four Ways from the hedge— and when they heard the shot, they went to investigate. By then, it was too late to do anything. They followed Josef. They believed he had the real papers—although he had fooled them once with a dummy set. It was not until Prince Josef recovered that the truth of the documents was known. They were in a safe deposit, where he had left them before going to seek Dawlish's help. A disloyal servant had told Otto where he was going, whom he hoped would give him the aid he needed.

Webber and Hanna stood their trial, charged as accessaries to Hal Scott's murder; and were found guilty and sentenced to death; the sentence was commuted to life imprisonment.

.    .    .    .    .

It was late spring when Tim Jeremy came again to Four Ways, fully recovered, and this time with his wife. Ted and his wife came too. The sun was out and the leaves were just covering the trees, gardeners were working, Maude and the daily woman were busy for the house party. In a way, it was a kind of house-warming, for the workmen had left Four Ways only the previous week, leaving everything as it had been before the storm had struck.

By coincidence, on that day the newspapers had carried the story that Prince Josef of Goetz was to have political asylum in this country.

So, Dawlish and his friends were talking. . . .

"Amazing little chap," Tim observed. "I didn't see how ñe pulled himself along to that room and challenged Otto. Must have been a sight. But I gather he's turned in all the jewels and what-have-you, kept enough to live on, and given the rest to the Red Cross and Unicef. Applause from both sides of the curtain. Ever discover *why* he came to see you, Pat, and what he hoped you would do?"

Dawlish was helping himself to a piece of cake, with sugar icing on top and whipped cream in the middle.

"Yes," he mumbled.

"Well, well. Why and what?"

"It couldn't have been more simple," Dawlish said. "He had his own personal agents and advisers, because he was never too happy about Otto and Emil, and he was in touch with one of our M.I.5 boys. The M.I.5 chap just couldn't help, and knew that, officially, no one would, but he told Josef that if he could get to me, I'd probably find a way to help. Apparently the mistake was due to my reputation for having no

truck with official channels, and sprang out of a job or two
we handled during the war.

"Josef was then sure that he would get no official help.

"He hadn't any friends—at least, none he could really
trust.

"So, he took a chance and came my way," Dawlish went
on, dreamily, and took a large bite of cake. "Mm. Not a bad
cook, my wife." He did not even wink at Felicity. "The thing
that really frightens me is what would have happened if I'd
already become Chief Copper."

Tim grinned.

Ted chuckled.

Their wives looked puzzled.

"Well, what——" began Mrs. Tim.

"Sweetheart," Tim said. "The answer couldn't be clearer.
He'd have thrown his hand in to get into any juicy job. And
if he ever looks like giving up his amateur status again, just
say 'Josef'."

"Or," suggested Ted, "say 'Hanna'."